Sally Forth

By

Jackie S. Hine

Published by New Generation Publishing in 2020

Copyright © Jackie S. Hine 2020

First Edition

The author asserts the moral right under the Copyright, Designs and Patents Act 1988 to be identified as the author of this work.

All Rights reserved. No part of this publication may be reproduced, stored in a retrieval system or transmitted, in any form or by any means without the prior consent of the author, nor be otherwise circulated in any form of binding or cover other than that which it is published and without a similar condition being imposed on the subsequent purchaser.

ISBN 978-1-78955-911-8

www.newgeneration-publishing.com

New Generation Publishing

CHAPTER 1

DESOLATION

She opened the door to her small cottage, the same door she had opened everyday for the last fifteen and a half years. Normally on a Friday evening Dave would have been waiting with a glass of merlot and a warm embrace. He used to spend the week away in London returning early on a Friday. He was never going to be there now, or ever again, he had gone, dead was such an emotive word it could not in anyway express the loss, the hurt, the sheer loneliness, the total finality of the outcome.

She threw her bag and school paraphernalia on the sofa and almost in one move managed to pour herself a very large glass of red wine and tune the radio to Classic fm. 'God, it was hot', the older colleagues at school remembered the summer of 76, her recollections were somewhat limited, she was only 7 at the time and as everybody knew childhood summers were always sunny! One thing was for certain however it *was* hot - if only it lasted for the rest of the summer. Term ended in another week and although there were no plans for a holiday, staying at home in her small Dorset village on the edge of the New Forest away from stroppy teenagers, back-biting colleagues, a moody Head who struggled constantly with the admin, the curriculum, the staff, would be a holiday in itself. She would of course have to visit her ageing parents and unless she agreed to stay for at least two nights her mother would be 'a bit put-out darling': father was more ambivalent and would spend most of the time at the local golf club while 'the girls' went shopping or whatever girls did -he was of the 'old school'.

Sally felt exhausted, she always felt like this, especially on a Friday and nearing the end of term, the heat certainly didn't help and seemed to sap her energy levels and, given that she had just spent two hours on the tennis court training the school tennis team she felt like retiring to bed. Instead she decided to indulge in her favourite passion, it was an odd passion for a female schoolteacher but she had started young and, as she got older and bolder, explored the many different types, tastes and sizes, she had now settled on a particular brand that she bought from her favourite shop. She had first come across the shop when taking her lunch break and since then had become very friendly with the husband and wife team that ran the tiny outlet, a stone's throw from the beach at Bournemouth. It was a cornucopia, a Pandora's box, an Aladdin's cave, she wondered what Dave would have thought if he had known of her love of smoking large hand made cigars, she almost felt guiltier now that he had gone than keeping the secret from him when he was alive.

She undressed and threw her damp sweaty clothes on the bed, went to the humidor where she kept her Honduran Churchill cigars, they were hand-made and large, 6 by 50, they weren't called 'Churchills' for nothing and the best thing was they were less than half the price of an equivalent Cuban, she had, she mused, become quite an aficionado over the years. This had become a ritual on most Fridays since Dave had died. If it was warm she would lay on her covered hammock on the patio, if it was cold she would sit in the living room with a blazing log fire although keeping the French doors wide open; she certainly didn't want visitors suspecting anything, it wouldn't somehow match her apparent demure persona and anyway it had always been a *secret* passion. Tonight, it was very warm and lying on her hammock puffing on her cigar and drinking a rather good 'Friday night' merlot would, she knew, relax her like nothing else. She expertly clipped the end of her cigar with the guillotine she had bought from 'her' shop and with deliberate care slowly lit the end making sure that all of it was alight before lying back on the hammock and taking that first taste. She let the rich mellow smoke fill her mouth before slowly exhaling, she had convinced herself that this was the way to lower her blood pressure although of course medical science would take issue, it certainly made *her* feel better. It gave her a feeling of inner peace, something a cigarette smoker could never understand. She had never smoked a cigarette in her life and didn't even like being around cigarette smokers, this was something altogether different, it wasn't an addiction, she could take it or leave it, it was as good as a three course meal, a good wine, why did she always try and justify it? As long as she could remember, her father had always smoked expensive Cubans and as a rebellious 13 year old would sneak a quick smoke when he left the room; as with most things that are really bad she initially found the taste quite disgusting but with time and perseverance began to like the taste and particularly the feeling smoking a good cigar gave her, it was a sort of panacea: so much so on her sixteenth birthday she 'borrowed' a large Cuban from her father's humidor and took it to the stables, there for the first time she enjoyed her first whole cigar, she couldn't believe that it took over an hour to smoke, from then on she decided that unless she could afford the best, she would do without. She spent many hours after then in the stables, it was a lonely passion and one she would have liked to share but didn't know anyone other than her father and that just wouldn't have been right. Her father never noticed that on occasion his cigars went missing, or if he did, he never said anything, although when she went off to university he gave her a magnificent hand made jewellery box he had brought back from the Caribbean. It was a very strange present for someone who wasn't particularly interested in rings and necklaces, but he said he couldn't resist it and knew it would come in useful. It had been her prized possession ever since and of course was now her humidor.

She looked down at her naked body. For a 39 year old she considered she was in reasonable shape, but she *was* a sports and modern languages teacher and unlike a lot of her friends, had never had children. Her calves were ok although slightly muscled, her thighs unremarkable but shaped well enough, her groin, a tangled triangle of very dark curly hair, her belly, flat. She took a sip of wine and with the remnants of the wine still lingering in her mouth took another long draw on her cigar, this time letting the smoke slowly curl from her lips, it made her eyes sting and she blinked a couple of times. What would Dave have said? She always suspected that he knew of her indulgence as there had been a couple of times, in a more enlightened period, when it was quite possible to enjoy a post-prandial cigar in a hotel after a decent meal, although she had only done this in his presence after quite a few drinks which he found quite amusing. 'God', how she loved to relax naked, in total privacy and with the warmth of the Sun on her body. She looked at the top of her legs, her big hairy mane was as always, thick and black just as Dave liked it; she'd seen no reason to change, she liked her hair, the hair on her head was thick and luscious just like her pubic hair, this new fashion of shaving and waxing, she didn't understand, it just wasn't natural, hair was as God intended. In the changing rooms with the girls at school after tennis was always fascinating, teenagers these days seemed far more sexually mature than she was at their age and she was amazed at what they did with their pubic hair: only Maria with the Italian/Swiss parents was similar to her and if it were at all possible her pubic hair was even darker and longer than Sally's and although Sally had never harboured lesbian thoughts, she was drawn to the foreign beauty. Since Dave died, she hadn't wanted another man and apart from the occasional bouts of self-abuse wasn't sure she would ever be able to give herself completely to someone else. Sex with Dave had been great, but her experience was limited to a brief romance at University in her last year with someone nearly as naïve as her. She poured herself another drink and completed her self examination. She had always considered her breasts to be her best feature, beautiful pert nipples and almost completely symmetrical 34 C's. She gently squeezed her left nipple and instantly felt the tissue stiffen between her fingers. Dave used to love her 'tits' and would spend time licking, touching and gently massaging them, touching herself now brought back distant memories of happier times.

Lying there with a cigar and drink in her hand took her to another plain, she still couldn't believe that she was worth about £1.6 million. It had come as a complete shock when the solicitor dealing with Dave's estate announced that she was to get a cheque for £1.32 million. His shares and considerable life assurance, which he had never spoken about, had been cashed in, she was without doubt a wealthy widow. They had never spoken about finance she was more than happy that they pooled his considerable salary and her more modest one; they never wanted for anything and spent without care. He had been generous and had bought the cottage for cash and on the day they married had transferred half to her. She first met him in a restaurant in Bangkok, a director of one of her father's companies had taken her there as a treat while she was on her 'walk-about' for a year after finishing university and introduced her to Dave, who was a very successful art director for an advertising company. He was fourteen years her senior, divorced, no children. He was tall, good looking and had an air and confidence about him, in an obtuse sought of way his manner reminded her very much of her own father. At the end of the night he asked where she was staying and insisted on travelling back in the taxi to her hotel. He wouldn't come in for a drink but asked her out the following evening on the pretext of showing her the delights of Bangkok: the next week was a whirlwind of dinners, lunches and sex! Bangkok was as far to the east as Sally managed to get, she ended up staying for a month. Dave only had six months of his contract left and returned to London in the spring. There was in her mind never any question from that first week that they would marry, even though he had said that the reason he didn't have any children with his first wife was because he couldn't - at 21 having children wasn't high up on her wish list. Her parents weren't keen on the age difference and the fact that Dave was divorced and, an art director, but were eventually won over by Dave's good manners, charisma and general charm. They married at her village church and then afterwards had the reception in a huge marquee on her parent's lawn.

She missed him as much now as when it happened. They never had time to say 'goodbye', he was very much alive when he left on that bright, frosty, Monday morning in January. An hour into her first lesson she had a message to see the headmaster in his office. She walked into the office and was met by icy stares from two police constables, a man and woman, she instantly thought she was in trouble as a result of the recent tennis tour when a few of her charges had got quite drunk and abused a couple of local dignitaries. Unfortunately, it was obvious that this was far more serious. The next few minutes were a blur of facts the only fact was that Dave was dead: he had been killed in a pile up on the M3. Looking back she couldn't remember the drive home or the next few days, her mother came down and gave her moral support but her entire life had been turned upside down, after three days her mother left making some poor excuse about an appointment at the hospital for her father, Sally didn't care and was glad to have her space back.

The school had been understanding and gave her as much time off as she wanted. She returned to work after half term but had not really come to terms with what had happened, or indeed, had time to grieve. Lying there she was beginning to feel very sorry for herself and the more she tried to put it out of her mind the more difficult it became, she had to shake herself out of this malaise even those at school had noticed that her personality had changed from 'bubbly' to morose, she felt they were even beginning to avoid making eye contact just in case they had to talk to her. This really couldn't continue she needed to change her routine. The smoke curled upwards in the still warm air and she could now taste the nutty, creamy coffee flavours the cigar was noted for: cigars and red wine were a great combination; it also had the effect of making her slightly light-headed, but not in a bad way. She could hear the strains of Vivaldi's Four Seasons escaping from the open window, in spite of her sadness it really was the most perfect way to unwind after a horrible week and, perhaps for the first time since his untimely death she realised that she must break the downward spiral she had been caught up in for the last six months and bring the mourning process to an end.

She stared at herself for sometime, before letting her right hand slowly settle between her legs, she let it rest there for a time, only occasionally exploring the parting of her lips with her middle finger: this wasn't an evening for doing anything quickly. She closed her eyes and imagined Dave staring down at her, something she had yearned for when he was alive but far too shy to ask, far too inhibited and in any case, he might have thought she was some sort of pervert. She had always been shy about exposing her body even though she was in good shape. Dave used to get annoyed when she turned her back on him in the shower and even on the hottest nights, she would always wear a nightie, even if later on he removed it. She was a private person and although lying here now naked, it was clearly on her terms. The warmth from the sun was still intense and it was more the French Riviera than the south coast of England. She was lucky that her cottage was right on the edge of the village and there was a field separating her from her nearest neighbour, the only sounds she could hear were the birds high up in the still evening air and Vivaldi's baroque masterpiece: very, very slowly she let her fingers explore her now moist, hairy opening and as only one can with such intimate knowledge of their own body started to stroke her clitoris with her index finger. With Dave it had often taken over an hour to reach a climax and more often than not, not at all, but as she lay there she imagined his body next to hers. Her hand left her groin and returned again to her nipples, both were now very erect and slightly swollen, she put her cigar between her very even white teeth and with both hands started to massage and rub her breasts and as she did, puffed on her cigar. She couldn't believe what she was doing and knew she was behaving more like a 'slut' than a school teacher but she was in the privacy of her own back yard and the more she did it, the more she liked it, but knew she was ever so slightly drunk. She took another large suck on her cigar and this time inhaled deeply, something she almost never did and, as the chemicals hit her bloodstream she had a head rush, very slowly she blew out the smoke from deep down in her lungs, a surreal feeling came over her and for the first time in nearly seven months she felt at peace with the world, certainly the urgency of the moment had left her. She put down her cigar and went inside for another bottle of wine, she knew now she was going to get hideously drunk, but really didn't care.

Sally went upstairs to the bathroom, showered and while she was still very soapy took the razor and with extreme care shaved her legs leaving her hairy underarms untouched, she liked the continental look, she had always been hairy, just like her mother: she stared down at her dark hairy mound and now looking at herself in the mirror she understood why Dave had always said that 'going down on her' was like a voyage of discovery, he never knew where he would end up. The hair went right round as far as her bottom and rather being put off like many men might have been, Dave loved her hirsuteness. Examining herself now reminded her, in some bizarre sort of way of her favourite horse, Simon, his mane was thick and strong and as she stroked and pulled her silky pubes she smiled at the oblique connection she had just made and in that instant knew she shouldn't drink anymore, but there was clearly no going back.

When she returned to her patio the sun had started to sink behind the Purbeck Hills, it was still warm and sticky and as she lay down again there was no holding back, this time with her legs slightly parted and her knees bent, she went straight to her thick black pubis and once more worked on herself. She loved the feeling of her newly shampooed soft fanny and felt very wet inside and with slow rhythmic movements and using both hands started to stroke and massage her pussy; she parted her lips, fingered her vagina and clitoris with evermore urgency and as the feelings started to build she became even more frantic, even fingering her bottom, she had never masturbated like this before, it was as if she was trying to penetrate her very soul. Her fingers were now all over her womanhood probing, squeezing, rubbing, she was totally surprised at her own roughness. She couldn't stop looking at herself and it was as if someone else was doing this to her, the juices were flowing and the little water droplets looked like little silver pearls in the black hairy triangle. When she eventually came it was like an internal explosion, it was unquestionably one of the most intense and dramatic orgasms she had ever experienced. She let out a loud moan as it seemed her whole body including her legs, lower belly and even her anal muscles shuddered to a climax and with each subsiding movement and spasm let her fingers gently withdraw, just now and again lightly touching her now very wet cunt. Sally started to sob, quietly at first and then with gathering emotion broke down and wept loudly, all the pent-up feelings of the last months coming out in one great outpouring of raw emotion.

Lying there for what seemed like an age she eventually regained her composure. As the sun disappeared completely from view leaving only a red glow in the west she carefully and expertly removed the old ash and relit the last third of her cigar and poured another glass of wine. With far less intensity than before she slowly drew on her cigar and without any other action on her part let the smoke very slowly escape from her thinly parted lips and go upwards in a vertical spiral in the now almost completely still air; sipping the last of the red wine there was absolutely no doubt that tomorrow she would have a headache, but she also knew it would dawn bright and warm in more ways than one. The evening had been a cathartic experience; tomorrow as the old cliché went was the first day of the rest of her life and although she didn't know how or why, she just knew it would be very different.

CHAPTER 2

THE SUMMER OF CONTENT

Sally knew that on Monday morning she needed to hand her notice in to the head. She would give a terms notice and although she was sure that, under the circumstances he would have accepted her leaving at the end of term she had always had a strong moral duty and owed it to her Spanish and French 'A' level students not to leave them at a critical time without adequate cover. He was very sympathetic and said the usual things about how marvellous she was and how difficult it would be to replace her, but he could see that she was adamant and knew that trying to get her to change her mind wasn't really an option, in any case he had seen it all before and was rather tired. She felt that a huge weight had been lifted from her shoulders; she had absolutely no idea of what she was going to do but knew that she had taken the first step in changing her life. The rest of the week passed off without incident, she said a tearful goodbye to the girls who were leaving and warned the next year's girls of what they were in for, if they were to get the grades they wanted and the universities they had selected. It was agreed with the headmaster that her departure at the end of the Autumn term would, for the time being, be kept secret. Usually by the end of the summer term Sally, like most of her peers, would be exhausted, but the sudden and quite unexpected turn of events left her feeling invigorated and re-energised. She decided that she wouldn't take a summer holiday but visit her parents for a week, (which would delight her mother) and spend the rest of the time in her garden that she had sadly neglected since Dave's hasty departure. One thing was for certain however; her life would never be the same again, even if she had absolutely no idea how she was going to spend it!

She decided that initially she wouldn't tell her parents of her decision as they would only worry: she had noticed, that as they approached their seventies, small things had become terribly important and although this didn't surprise her about her mother, she had always considered her father to be 'bomb proof', a very successful entrepreneur, a 'bon viveur', just an all round solid chap. Sally rang them that evening and arranged to go for a week the last week of her holidays, her mother was delighted and started reeling off all the places they would go to.

"Quite frankly darling I thought when your father retired he would spend a bit more quality time with me, Bristol has changed so much, the dock area is full of lovely restaurants but he seems to live and eat at the golf club, it will be great to just do girlie things for a week."

Sally wasn't sure in retrospect whether this seemed like a good idea, but the deed was done and there was no going back and she had always got on very well with her mother, which was just as well, being an 'only' child.

The first week of the summer holiday started dull and it seemed the weather had broken and gone back to a typical pattern of sunshine and showers. She didn't mind too much as she always spent the first week preparing her course work for the next term and doing things she should have done the previous term but was always too busy. She liked to do it this way as it meant the rest of the summer was hers to do with as she wanted. By Thursday she was feeling rather bored with schoolwork and decided to go shopping for a bit of light relief, in any case she needed new trainers for tennis and she was meeting her best friend Izzie at the tennis club that night. Thursday night was club night and there weren't many Thursdays during the summer months when both wouldn't turn up. Paul and Izzie had been Dave and Sally's closest friends and she knew how important they had been for her after 'the accident'. They had two teenage boys who were away at boarding school, so during term time they were effectively childless. They first met at the tennis club, Izzie was new to the area and they immediately 'hit it off', it wasn't long before they got together as a foursome and although there was an age gap between Paul and Dave, they shared many interests, the most important were golf and squash. Dave introduced Paul to both the golf and squash clubs and barely a week went by when they wouldn't all meet up.

They had gone away for weekends together and had become very close: there was not a lot that was 'off limits' and they would be terribly rude to each other and tease each other unmercilessly, there was however never any physical sexual impropriety even if sometimes their drunken discussions late at night got slightly out of hand. Sally had never really thought of Paul in a sexual way although she had become slightly curious about Paul's willy ever since Dave came back the first night after playing squash with him and told Sally that Paul had the biggest cock he had ever seen. Bearing in mind Dave, like most chaps, who played a lot of sport, had seen thousands of cocks during his lifetime, this seemed to Sally rather impressive. The first time they met after that revelation was a week later and Sally couldn't take her eyes off Paul's groin area. There was, quite clearly, a large 'thing' going down his right leg that seemed to Sally to be half-way to his knee. She looked up only to find Paul looking at her, she immediately felt the colour rise to her cheeks and she averted her gaze, never again did she deliberately look there although subconsciously she often found herself gazing at his manhood.

"Hi, Sally."

It was Izzie, she always looked the same, immaculately dressed, even in tennis gear, never a hair out of place, make-up, just so.

"Hi, Izzie, had a good week?"

"Not bad, although I have had to go in all week this week as everyone seems to be on holiday."

Izzie worked in a charity shop three days a week. Sally was never quite sure what Paul did other than he had a very high- powered job with a financial services company based in Bournemouth. She did know that he must have earnt a lot to keep two boys at a rather good boarding school and as long as she had known them, Izzie had never had a paid job. Izzie went on to the court and started to practise her serves, hitting the balls with a surprising amount of power considering she was as slight a build as Sally. They were extremely keen rivals and whilst Izzie may have hit the ball harder, Sally had a range of shots that were far superior. They were of a very similar standard and normally the games would go with serve until one broke through. Even though they were rivals it never spilled into any unpleasantness, unlike some of the bitches who played there. They were also great doubles partners and had won the club championships twice in the last three years although neither of them ever getting beyond the semi finals in the singles.

It was five all in games and they seemed to be heading for a stalemate.

"Shall we call it a day, I'm not used to this work malarkey, I think I'd rather get changed and go for a drink, how about you?"

Sally could have gone on but could see Izzie was genuinely tired. They showered in the private cubicles and both had towels wrapped around them when they appeared back in the changing room. They were even similar about their modesty. Some of the women, especially the young ones, would parade around showing off everything they had, much to both their annoyance. Izzie had a very neat figure and when she dropped her towel to get dressed Sally noticed what was quite obviously a love bite on her back.

"God Izzie, what's that all about? I though you well past that sort of thing."

"Past what sort of thing?"

"You have a love bite on your back."

"Shush!"

In a whispered voice and clearly embarrassed Izzie said she would explain all when they had a drink.

Sitting outside the local bar with a couple of gin and tonics they were discussing some of the women at the tennis club, now it was their turn to be bitchy but there really were some awful people.

"Come on then tell me how you got that mark on your back, are you having an affair?"

"You must be joking I'm too worn out Paul is insatiable he never used to be like it, I'm sure he's taking something. When we were in bed the other night he said he wanted to tell me something that turned him on," she hesitated……

"Go on, you can't leave me up in the air."

"He said he fancied having a threesome with another woman."

"Is that all, most men fantasise about it, Dave was always mentioning it."

"No, but honestly Sally he meant it, I know if I agreed he would sort something out. I told him in no uncertain terms that no hooker was either going to share my bed, my husband, or me come to that. I couldn't have been more definite, and he could see I was annoyed. I would have thought it would have put him off having sex but it didn't and when we did …...wow! Whether it was his thoughts or the fact he had told me, it was like before we got married, I'm certain the boys must have heard us. It wasn't until I washed my hair the next day, I saw what he had done to my back, I just hope he wasn't with anyone when he got my text the next morning. Anyway, enough about my mucky husband, have you met anybody yet?"

Izzie knew she hadn't as she would have been the first one she would tell. Her silence confirmed her assumption,

"Come on, it's been eight months now, you will end up an old spinster."

"I'm frightened and it's still very early, Dave and I were so close and had such a great time I just couldn't commit to anyone."

"You don't have to commit to anyone just have a good time, you must know a few eligible single men?"

"All the 'single' men I know are either cheating on their wives, old and ugly, both or gay. Doesn't Paul know anyone at work that he could recommend; I almost feel I would have to know someone before I could sleep with them. You know my history I have only slept with two people in my life. God, Izzie I have only felt or seen six cocks in my entire life and one of those I saw was my dads when I walked in the bathroom by mistake one day, I don't know out of the two of us who was the most embarrassed, he always locked the door after that."

"You really are a sad case, you are only nearly 40, didn't you know that 40 is the new 30. By the way it's your 40th a week on Saturday, are you still having a family do?"

"Oh, I didn't tell you did I? Father hasn't been too well of late and I am now only going for lunch. To tell the truth I am quite looking forward to having a night in with a few DVD's and a large bottle of Red."

She very nearly said "and a Cohiba Esplendido," which would have been a bit of a shock for Izzie, although Izzie would probably not have known what one was.

"That's settled then, Paul cooks for me on a Saturday, the boys are with Paul's mum, I'll get a few DVD's in and we can all get drunk and you can stay with us for the night. There is no way my best friend in all the world is spending her 40th birthday alone."

Sally said she would, although she would still quite have liked a night on her own. She was going out with a few of her teacher friends on the Wednesday after the A level results had come out, Friday, her gay friends John and Andy insisted that they take her to their favourite Italian, Saturday she would be driving to Bristol to meet her parents for lunch and now Saturday evening she would be at Paul and Izzies, well at least since she had decided to 'change her life', she couldn't complain too much about her social life.

The next week went so quickly, she went out with the teachers on Wednesday and realised after spending a boring night listening to them talk 'shop' that she had definitely made the right decision. John and Andy behaved like a couple of old queers, which in fact is what they were, but as always, she had a fantastic night and 'camped it up' with them at the restaurant. The lunch with her parents was as she expected, predictable although she did notice that her father was quieter than normal. When she got home from Bristol she really felt that she could do without going to see Paul and Izzie and wished she'd 'stuck to her guns', she wasn't someone to let anyone down however to be honest seeing her best friends would make a welcome change, if nothing else at least she would have a laugh, something that was never in much evidence when she was with her parents, it wasn't that they were miserable, there was just a large generation gap when it came to a sense of humour.

By the time she had showered, had a quick drink, she felt invigorated and ready to enjoy her 40th birthday party with her best friends, her only regret was that she would be going alone. Dinner was from one of her favourite 'up-market' food shops and was superb, Paul had managed to cook it in line with the instructions, but the star of the show was the copious amounts of Bollinger champagne that they had bought in her honour. Paul insisted on clearing away and the two girls carried on drinking and getting quite giggly. Paul suddenly appeared in the doorway.

"Have you asked her then?"

She looked at Izzie, there was a complete look of bewilderment on her face. She tried to protest but Sally cut her short.

"I don't want to know, but I really think I should go home."

"Please don't, he's just drunk, go on have another drink he will be snoring in a few minutes."

Izzie poured another brandy and handed it to Sally.

"I told you he wasn't joking, he's completely obsessed with the idea, I didn't think for one minute he'd suggest you joined us."

"Well at least I'd know him, I shan't forget my 40th birthday in a hurry, will I?"

"I really didn't know anything about it, honestly. I realise that the four of us were very close and we used to joke about sleeping with each other but that's as far as we got. I did think however if we had ever gone on a summer holiday together without the kids something may have happened, as I know Paul used to fancy you."

This was a complete surprise to Sally, he had always teased her, but she thought it was just his way, as she had seen him similarly tease other women when they had all been out together. She knew that Dave fancied Izzie because one of his little games when they used to lie in bed together was him asking Sally to describe her in minute detail, right down to the colour of her pubic hair. She would make it up, describing how Izzie had a mass of hair like her because she knew it would turn him on: in fact the reverse was quite true, Izzie used to keep her pubes very neat, no particular style, just very short. If Sally had been braver she would have asked Dave to describe Paul's enormous cock but that wasn't her way and in any case she doubted whether Dave would have been very forthcoming, she surmised that blokes probably didn't like talking about other bloke's cocks, especially when they were a lot bigger!

She wondered if Paul would be asleep now or whether he would have his mammoth cock in his hand. She looked at Izzie knowing how shocked she would be if she could read her mind, she was also quite shocked to think it had crossed her own mind.

"Do you want another brandy?"

Sally did, as she was now on a roll and would have absolutely loved a cigar, but this was clearly not on offer and there had been enough shocks for one night.

"Go on have another one, it is your 40th and I feel I need one to help me recover from shock. The nonsense of it is that he didn't seem that drunk, did he?"

She poured another large brandy and handed it to Sally.

"Right Sally, one way or another I am going to halt your sex drought, it's not normal and Dave wouldn't have wanted you to become a nun."

Sally giggled out loud as she pictured Dave lifting her habit and giving her one. She was becoming very silly and so was Izzie. They started to both giggle at the thought of Dave lifting Sally's habit.

The door opened and Paul was standing stark bollock naked with the most enormous erection Sally had ever seen.

I thought if 'Mohammed wouldn't come to the mountain, then the mountain would come to Mohammed'.

He was quite drunk, and Sally was amazed that he could sustain an erection, whenever Dave got really drunk it nearly always ended up in disappointment, disappointment that is for Sally as he would normally fall asleep.

"My God Paul what are you thinking of?"

With that Sally became quite hysterical, sniggering uncontrollably, she didn't know if it was the drink, his cock, the bizarre situation that was unfolding, it was all becoming a bit unreal. Paul moved towards Sally.

"Come on then Sally you know you want to touch it."

Sally really did she looked at Izzie who looked back at her. Izzie was giggling, probably out of nervousness; neither of them knew what to do.

"Have I got to stand to attention all night before anyone does anything?"

Completely out of the blue and then out of character Izzie stood up, turned out the main light leaving only the light on from the hall, she then stripped naked and moved towards her husband, there were now two naked people in the room and one fully clothed. The giggling had stopped and Sally felt isolated, an unwilling voyeur, it was as if she was watching it on T.V. Paul sat down on the floor with his wife beside him, she very slowly started to wank his massive circumcised cock while he indulged her in mutual masturbation. Sally could hear the light strains of Ella Fitzgerald in the background and they seemed to be wanking in time with the music. Sally either had to stay or go, if she stayed she could go to bed and hoped it would all be forgotten in the morning, if she went, apart from the fact it was a mile walk, it was unlikely she would be able to face them again.

"You always used to look at it, you might as well see it close up in the flesh."

They shifted their position, Izzie mounted her husband sitting on his face and allowing him to lick inside her. Neither could now see Sally. Sally looked at his erect prick and decided she would stay and not go to bed. She slipped out of her clothes, out of site of both of them and sat down, her legs either side of Pauls. She needed both hands, it reminded her of holding her hockey stick and with deliberate strokes she moved her hands up and down. Her eyes had become accustomed to the half light and she could now clearly make out the great purple circumcised helmet, she looked at him, she knew that before long she would force him inside her. His shaft was shaved smooth and there was only a fuzz of hair on his pubic bone, his balls were round and large, she cupped them with her hands and moved her mouth towards his lovely 'head'. She had to open her mouth wide to accommodate his tip and as she did, it reminded her of the first time she had tried a very large cigar, this felt as good but in a very different way. She tried to swallow his monster but could only manage a few inches without gagging, she let it rest in her mouth using her lips and teeth, gently squeezing and sucking, she took it out again and ran her tongue around the circumcised rim, she drew on it as she would her cigar while her hands massaged his lovely big spherical balls. Both Paul and Izzie were moaning, and she could see her friend writhing up and down on her husband's face. She couldn't believe what she was doing, she wondered what Dave would think although, quite honestly she couldn't have cared less, one thing was for certain, she had well and truly exorcised his ghost.

She reluctantly moved her mouth away and sat astride him, she wasn't surprised that his cock easily reached her breasts and for a few moments she forced the monster between her tits, using his pink end to stroke her now, large, stiff pink nipples. Very, very carefully, she positioned herself over him, having to hold on to her friend as she did so and then began to lower her now dripping wet fanny over his huge purple prick. She took her weight on her knees and now with both hands free, used one to open her lips as wide as she could and with the other, guide him into her. She groaned with the initial discomfort as he filled her from side to side and she began the initially tortuous, but wonderful feeling of having him inside her, eventually after what seemed an age he slid fully home and Sally very carefully moved up and down, riding his shaft, it felt that her whole body was filled by him. She could feel a pulse inside her and didn't know whether it was hers or his, her breathing was laboured as it took effort to slide up and down his long thick shaft. He began to thrust in time with her and together they rode along in unison. Sally was aware that Izzie was no longer on top but at his side and watching her fuck her husband. Any inhibitions had long since gone and Sally didn't care, she *did* care about getting pregnant though and with what was probably her last remaining sensible thought she removed herself as his thrusting became more urgent and once again took him in her mouth. He came almost immediately, and Sally felt the warm semen hit the back of her throat, she removed her mouth and grabbing him with both hands again she finished him off, covering her face, tits and hair with the last drops of his cum. That was something she would never have let Dave do! She wasn't finished though and seemingly without a care in the world she lay back and in full view of her friends stroked her hairy mound with the same passion as a few weeks earlier, neither of them attempted to intervene but stared at the huge black mass of wet tangled hair that stretched from her pussy to her anus. With a sudden surge she came, not once, but twice in quick succession, it was as if she had been saving herself for that moment. Her whole body shook and she let out a cry of pure unadulterated ecstasy and then lay very still. Without any prior warning she felt Paul's tongue enter her still wet, hot, hole, she wasn't sure whether she was ready for this new assault, his touch firm and demanding. She could see Izzie sitting in the big armchair watching them, she was touching herself, but at no time did she make any attempt to join them, which Sally was pleased about, she didn't know whether she would ever be ready for a completely physical relationship with her best friend. She eventually heard her friend softly whimper and, as if it was a sign to end, Paul withdrew and turned over on to his back, his cock now limp and lifeless and laying on his leg looking, for all the world, Sally thought, like a beached whale. Sally slowly got up and without looking at either of them went upstairs and had a shower.

She stood in the shower letting the hot water revive her, the water running off her body in great rivulets; she took the shower head and showered her legs and pubic area soaping her pussy until there was a great froth that covered her from navel to thighs, it was as if she was trying to deny what had just happened by washing it away. She washed her hair and breasts making sure any remnants of Paul's cum went away with the dirty water. What she had just participated in and seen, was slowly beginning to dawn on her, she was unsure of her feelings. She dried herself and left the bathroom, downstairs she could hear her best friends having dirty, filthy, noisy sex: there was no need for her to join them again, she knew she wasn't required. She closed her bedroom door quietly and lay down.

Slipping quietly from their house the next morning she walked the mile or so home in a light drizzle, it felt good to feel it on her face, it was still very early and the only person she saw was the paper boy. When she got home, she walked up the stairs and went back to bed. She was woken by the telephone she wasn't immediately aware of where she was but suddenly last nights events came flooding back. Without looking, she knew who would be calling and was afraid to answer, although she knew at some stage she had to face them again.

"Morning, Sal."

Not many people got away with calling her 'Sal'.

"What time is it?"

"12 o clock ish I think, Paul and I have only just got up."

There was unmistakably a pause while Izzie waited for her friend to say something.

Sally hesitated not knowing what to say.

"Me and Paul are going to have a bit of breakfast we would really like you to join us."

"I have to wash my hair and I promised to pop round to see a friend," she lied.

"Go on, please come round we both want to see you."

Sally knew she had to face them sometime and leaving it would only make things worse.

"O.K. but give me an hour I haven't got up yet."

Izzie opened the door.

"Sally, I"

Sally cut her short

"You lied to me, you told me you knew nothing about it, nobody changes their mind that quickly."

"Honestly Sally all I said to Paul was that if I ever had another woman in my bed with him it would have to be you, because you were my best friend. I only said it to him to shut him up, I had absolutely no idea what he was planning, but it certainly explains a couple of things. The two women looked at each other, for a moment there was awkwardness, then Sally put her arms around her and hugged her.

"Izzie, I couldn't bear to lose you both as friends, where's Paul?"

"He's hiding in the shed."
"For God's sake tell him to come and see me."

They sat and had brunch in the garden. They all agreed that it had been a rather strange but interesting night and as Sally said.

"If I was going to break my duck?"

"Fuck, more like." said Paul.

"It was with the best two people in the world. I think though your friendship is worth more to me, it has to be a one-off."

They all nodded in agreement, but Sally wasn't the only one feeling that it wouldn't be, although just in case it was, she promised herself that she would go to Ann Summers in the morning and buy the biggest dildo she could find.

CHAPTER 3

LAST OF THE SUMMER WINE

The rest of the summer holiday seemed to fly by, Paul and Izzie took the boys camping in France and Sally went to stay with her parents for the last week of the holidays, although, she didn't quite manage the full 7 days. She was rather pleased that she couldn't see her friends and although there was no obvious awkwardness, she felt that the 3 weeks enforced separation would do them all good. She couldn't however get the events of that night from her mind: it didn't help that she had, as she had promised, bought the biggest dildo Ann Summers sold and nicknamed it 'Paul' and since that fateful coupling had, on more than one occasion, in the privacy of her back garden, laying on her hammock, extended her range of pleasures by including 'Paul'.

As often happens the weather in the last few weeks of the school holidays had reverted to the typical English summer - sunshine and showers, and as soon as the school term was about to begin the whole of Southern England was blessed with the most glorious 'Indian Summer'. On the last night before the term commenced Sally was with 'Paul' enjoying the last few hours of freedom when the door bell rang: it was very unusual that she ever had visitors unannounced and was debating whether to answer it or not when the bell rang again with more urgency this time. She quickly hid 'Paul', slipped on her baggy pantaloons and tee-shirt and answered the door: it was Izzie.

"Sorry for barging in, I would have rung, but I was passing anyway and thought I would pop in for a cup of tea."

Apart from a brief telephone conversation when Izzie got back from France they hadn't really spoken much and under normal circumstances Sally would have welcomed catching up with her friend, but somehow, she was annoyed that her 'lotus eating' had been disturbed. She was however always polite and asked her in.

"Cup of tea, or glass of red?"

"O.K. you talked me round but only a small one as I am driving."

They sat in silence for a moment before they both spoke at once.

"No, go on, tell me all about your holiday."

"We had an absolutely fantastic time, none of us wanted to come home but I didn't really come around to talk about our holiday. Paul and I had a long time to discuss things when we were in France and I don't quite know how to put this but………"

"But what?"

"But we would rather like to do it again."

Although Sally knew perfectly well what she was referring to she made her spell it out.

"Do what again?"

"Come on Sally don't make this anymore difficult for me than it already is. Paul and I want to involve you again like we did a few weeks ago. Sex between us has been brilliant, even better than when we first got together and I know what we are both thinking of, when we are…you know… doing it. My God, on holiday we couldn't get rid of the boys to the pool quickly enough. God knows what the Germans in the next tent to ours must have thought."

"I don't know what to say"

"Look, don't say anything, I promised Paul I would talk to you and I have, I'll go now, I promise whatever you decide, it won't ruin our friendship."

Sally was pleased to show her the door, she really didn't know what to think but she knew she was wet at the thought. She went straight outside, got 'Paul' from his hiding place, slipped her pantaloons down to her ankles and as she had done a few weeks ago with the real thing, opened her pussy lips to accept him. With great care she introduced him once again to her vagina and with slow deliberation pushed him all the way in, she gasped as he slid into her. She wanked him up and down, withdrawing him half way before sliding him back into her and as she did so she squeezed her vaginal muscles as if she was trying to ring life out of the dead thing that was inside her, she only wished it was the real thing. It didn't take long before she came, not in great rasping breathes as before, but nonetheless with a slow release of pleasurable, but ever subsiding spasms. She lay there unable to move with 'Paul' still buried deep inside, very slowly she withdrew the lifeless monster and put it on the floor. She had become a shameless hussy, but she didn't care, her only regret was the fact she hadn't been like it with Dave: how their sex life might have been very different? She looked to the heavens as if she was trying to seek help and advice, but all she could see were the bright stars; there was an autumnal chill in the air and laying there she felt the cool air on her wet fanny, she pulled up her pants and knew there were decisions she had to make. One thing was for certain, since Dave had died her character had altered, or perhaps it was just that life was far too short, and she had a lot of living left to do. She just couldn't believe the person she had become. She lit a 'Churchill', poured herself another glass of wine and thought very dark and dirty thoughts.

There was an announcement on the first day of term that she would be leaving at Christmas due to personal reasons. The staff who had previously kept their distance suddenly started talking to her again and she felt that things were back to normal; she actually considered taking back her notice but knew deep down that this wasn't really an option. At a parent's meeting half way through term, she was approached by Maria's parents who were worried that their daughter wouldn't get the grades she needed to get into Cambridge and asked if she would give her extra tuition until her 'A' levels the next summer. Sally said that she would consider it. She clearly didn't need the money and although she hadn't planned on travelling until the following September, wasn't sure if she wanted the hassle, however, she liked Maria and couldn't really find a reason to say 'no'. It was agreed that Maria would start with Sally the third Sunday of January and if everything went according to plan would have a two - hour lesson every weekend until she took her 'A' levels.

The term drifted on and although she did her best for the students Sally knew her heart wasn't in it and couldn't wait for the end of term. She saw Izzie a few times at the tennis club, but nothing was mentioned of their previous conversation, life just seemed to settle down into a familiar pattern. Paul had been seconded to the Zurich office which meant he was away all week and as a result, Sally kept her distance at weekends. They had never really 'lived in each other's pockets' so it wasn't unusual that Sally didn't see them at weekends. When Dave had been alive it was more of a weekday relationship, as they all played sport together and only occasionally would get together at weekends. Anyway, she felt they should have some space and at the moment it suited her not to have to make a decision, it was, she thought a complication that she didn't need and for the time being her needs could be met by 'Paul' she kept under her bed!

Christmas was approaching and even though Sally had made her decision to leave six months earlier she hadn't given any real thought to what she was going to do. Initially she fancied the idea of travelling, but travelling on your own wasn't such great fun and although she might meet people, her thoughts were coming around to the idea of a 'project' of some sort, she might even consider doing some charity work in a far flung place. She had, however, decided that once Christmas was over she would start investigating the possibilities for her future, although there was no hurry and she had definitely decided to take at least six months off and enjoy the summer at home.

Her mother kept in touch every week and Sally felt a little guilty that it was always her mother who phoned her but it had been like that for as long as she could remember and that was just the way it was.

"What are you doing for Christmas, darling?"

It was, of course a rhetorical question and before Sally could speak, she continued.

"You will of course be coming to stay with Daddy and me?"

Once again it wasn't really a question but a statement of fact. Sally and Dave had always gone to her parents for Christmas Eve and Christmas Day returning early on Boxing Day to relax at home. This was the first Christmas that Sally would be without Dave and even the thought of her mother's constant chatter didn't stop Sally from having a nice warm feeling about spending Christmas with her family.

At the end of term the staff gave her a leaving party, she thought she ought to be emotional, but she wasn't, she knew that she had made the right decision regardless of what she would do in the future. They bought her a peach tree for her garden which she found a bit bizarre especially as they knew of her intention to go travelling, although presumably it would still be there when she returned. She said her goodbyes and promised to keep in touch, going through the gates for the last time was a good feeling. Izzie had asked Sally round to celebrate her 'retirement' and Sally found herself looking forward to seeing them both again, it had been a couple of weeks since she had seen Izzie and with Paul's enforced absence it must have been over a month since she had seen him. They made her very welcome and had bought her a leaving present, a beautiful cut glass crystal decanter.

"We know you like wine and as you will have far more time to drink it now, we thought it would be a nice gift."

"You make me sound like an alcoholic. I think I will have to watch myself, it's so easy to open a bottle especially when you're on your own and it barely gets light all day. God, I hate the winter, I can't wait for the summer to come."

Izzie had prepared a simple supper of lasagne and a tiramisu for afters she had always been a great cook but normally let Paul cook at weekends. It was a bit of a hobby, but he was nowhere near as accomplished as his wife, but his wife, being the lovely person she was, and their many dinner guests, would always tell him how good dinner was. Sally and Dave had had some very forgettable dinners and although Dave would rib his friend, Sally was always more circumspect. They spoke about everything except the one subject that had been eating away at Sally. She was glad they didn't mention the events of a few months earlier and assumed that her silence and lack of response to Izzie was an end to the matter. Paul was off to Zurich the next day quite early and Izzie was picking up the boys from school for the holidays, so at 9.30pm Sally said that she was very tired and a felt a bit emotional about leaving her job and drove the mile or so home. She drove home with very mixed emotions, leaving her job was the least of it. She was beginning to think more about Dave again, perhaps it was the time of year, perhaps....... oh just bloody perhaps. As she got out of the car she felt a tear trickle down her cheek: she locked the door behind her and went upstairs to bed.

Christmas was spent with her parents, for the first time she noticed that they were getting old, since they had both turned seventy it had suddenly seemed to age them. Her mother probably faired better than her father who seemed to have suddenly slowed down, apparently according to her mother he had bought himself an electric buggy for his golf rounds, saying that he could no longer walk all the way around 18 holes without getting out of breath. Sally actually stayed all of Boxing Day much to her mother's delight, she didn't fancy spending it on her own, this time last year Dave and her had gone to the local hunt meet and then had lunch at one of their favourite village pubs. The memory was still very clear, and Sally knew that spending the day sitting at home looking at his empty chair was not a good recipe for happiness. She knew it was going to be hard enough the few days between then and New Years Eve which she was spending at Paul and Izzies, who always hosted a big party. Never mind she was going out with her gay friends, John and Andy, they would be a laugh, they always were.

The New Year's Eve bash at Paul and Izzies was a lonely affair, everybody tried their best, but the events of a year ago remained very raw and real. It could be a very lonely time of year. They all got very drunk and when the clock heralded in the New Year it was as if she was a magnet, it was as if everybody sensed her loneliness and descended on her, hugging and kissing her. Paul was the first to arrive and gave her a full kiss on the lips slipping his tongue into her mouth. This was not that unusual when he was drunk and he'd done it many times before, Dave always knew because Sally used to tell him and he found it quite amusing, never taking offence. Sally wondered if Dave ever kissed Izzie like that. What happened next she didn't expect, he whispered very loudly in her ear and she was sure everyone in the room must have heard.

"Come around a week on Saturday for dinner, the boys are back at school and Izzie and I want you to."

There was absolutely no ambiguity about the invitation and even in her inebriated state she heard herself saying 'yes'.

She arrived with some trepidation, taking a box of chocolates. Paul was in the kitchen cooking his masterpiece. Izzie looked fantastic, she had a red dress with buttons at the front, she was not wearing a bra and her cleavage was still impressive even so.

"I have been banned from the kitchen, I haven't got a clue, come in the lounge and have a drink."

Sally needed a stiff one if the evening was going to end as she anticipated. Izzie sensing the same, poured out two enormous gin and tonics.

"I have to be honest Sal, this isn't the first one of the day."

Paul came into the lounge a few minutes later and announced that dinner was ready.

There was, considering what Sally expected later, a very relaxed atmosphere and she began to think she had misunderstood the 'invitation'. Dinner was superb, Paul had excelled himself and the conversation flowed as liberally as the wine, but there was still no mention of anything untoward about to happen. By the end of the meal they were all rather silly. Suddenly Paul stood up and it was obvious before he even opened his mouth what he was thinking.

"I will tidy everything away why don't you two girls go and have a shower I will be up in ten minutes."

There was certainly no misunderstanding now; it was as if it was the most natural thing in the world to do after a great meal with your friends. She couldn't back out now and didn't want to; this is what she had come for.

They went to the main bathroom where there was a magnificent walk in power shower, Sally had always wanted one but it would have been quite impossible to have one fitted into her much smaller cottage. Izzie asked Sally if she would soap her back as it was always nice if someone else reached those parts you couldn't. Sally took some shower gel and worked it into her friend's shoulders and down her spine stopping just short of her bottom; she felt there was an expectation for her to continue, but she didn't. Izzie turned around and took the gel from Sally and started to massage her back, her hands reached under Sally's hairy armpits and worked up a lather, as she did she let her hands touch, but not fondle, Sally's breasts. The water came out of the sides and tops in great powerful jets and both girls could sense the water stinging and seducing every inch of their bodies, it was a very sensuous feeling. They got out and dried, wrapping a towel around themselves; they looked at each other and giggled at the ridiculous modesty of what they had just done, considering what they were just about to do.

Paul was already in bed and although he was covered in a quilt there was still an unmistakeable bulge half-way down.

"Come on girls, I thought you had been washed away."

Both girls slipped off their towels and got into bed, one each side. No sooner had they lay down when Paul threw back the quilt and went down on Sally. All Sally could see was Paul's curly black hair and it reminded her of her own. She could feel his tongue and lips on her and wondered whether *he* felt, it was a 'voyage of discovery'. He was quite expert, although much rougher than she was used to with Dave he made little darting movements with his tongue which she could feel at the entrance to her vagina, he then used his lips to caress hers and explored every inch, even as far as that little delicate area of skin that is the boundary between the fanny and bum, the bit she could never remember the name of, even if it had a name? Her hands now started to play with her breasts, and she could feel her urgency as she twisted and pulled at her nipples. She wondered what her friend was doing; she couldn't see her but could hear the dull throb of a battery motor and could picture the scene. Sally was heading very quickly for an orgasm when Paul suddenly stopped what he was doing: he grabbed her and turned her over, as he did so he pulled her towards the bottom of the bed and spread eagled her legs so she ended up with one either side of the corner, she was surprised and shocked at his roughness, the next moment he forced himself deep into her. Perhaps because of her practise with 'Paul' at home, or perhaps because of the position, but regardless he managed to smoothly slide in without any opposition until he completely filled her. His movements weren't considerate like before but with a strength and roughness that she found both shocking and exciting in equal measure, within a very short time she came, but as she was taking the last bit of him he suddenly withdrew, he immediately turned his attention to his wife with the same roughness he had fucked Sally: he drew his wife's legs apart and rested one on each of his shoulders, exposing her ripe opening. He forced himself upon her and clasping his hands around the back of her neck he drew her towards him so he could get maximum penetration. Unlike Sally however, she was equal to the challenge and they both became animals, scratching, clawing, grunting, moaning, shouting and swapping expletives. Their movements were violent, and Sally could only watch in a detached way, the same way that on occasion she had watched a porn movie with Dave. She slipped off the bed and picked her clothes up from the bathroom and made her way to the front door, she could hear their cries and the creaking of the mattress and springs and knew they wouldn't even have been aware of her leaving. For a brief moment she almost felt sorry for the Germans!

She opened her front door, went to the kitchen and put the kettle on: drinking her tea she was totally unsure of her feelings, she almost felt that she had been violated and used and began to wonder whether her friend wasn't more involved in organising the ménage a trois than she was letting on. She wasn't sure how she should feel, she almost felt like a victim, but why should she? Sally had entered the contract knowing they were all consenting adults, now, soon as it didn't turn out to be the gentle sex she used to enjoy with Dave, she was running scared. God knows, she had enjoyed it the first time and in retrospect this time could have been even more exciting and fantastic had she fully participated, it was just so unexpected and different. Sally needed to gather her thoughts, she certainly couldn't take the moral high ground, she needed time to think and rationalise her emotions. Although, the last thing she would be doing in the morning would be answering the phone!

CHAPTER 4

A NEW AWAKENING

Maria had just passed her test and drove over the few miles from town, she arrived, as agreed at 10am on Sunday, 17th January. Sally let her in and showed her into the dining room as there was a decent sized table where they could spread their books and papers.

"Would you like a coffee before we start?"

Sally brought in a tray of coffee with a plate of biscuits and offered Maria a chocolate digestive.

"No thanks, I am trying to lose weight"

For the first time since Maria arrived Sally looked at her properly, she was really striking. Her long black hair was scraped into some sort of loose bun arrangement with a large clip holding it all together exposing her slender neck – she certainly couldn't be described as fat, or even big. Maria sensing that Sally was requiring some sort of explanation said that her mother's sisters who still lived in Italy were prone to putting on weight in their early thirties and she didn't want to take after them.

They spent two hours conversing in Spanish, only occasionally did Sally have to correct her grammar or pronunciation, she really was very good. Maria was already bilingual at the age of two as both her parents spoke Italian at home, but she needed three 'A' grades if she was sure to get into Cambridge to study modern languages. Sally was in no doubt that she would achieve a grade 'A' and began to wonder why her father had insisted on the extra lessons. She was rather glad, as since she had left the school at Christmas, she felt a remoteness and this way somehow kept her in touch with what she had lost and anyway, Maria had always been her favourite. If ever Sally had a daughter, she would have wanted her to be like Maria.

She continued to play tennis with Izzie most Thursdays, and nothing was ever mentioned. There was no real difficulty between them although she could sense things weren't quite normal. Sally thought she may have dreamed of what had happened. In mid February they were having their customary drink after playing tennis when Izzie suddenly announced that they were moving to Zurich.

"When did you know?"

"Well it's been on the cards for some time and just after the Christmas holidays it was confirmed. We couldn't say anything at the time until we had told our families and the boys, in fact the night you came for dinner we were going to tell you then, but you went rather quickly. Look Sal, we felt really bad about what happened and Paul and I have argued about it ever since."

For the first time Sally didn't know how to respond but she knew the air had to be cleared, she couldn't bear that her best friends went off to Zurich 'under a cloud'.

"To tell the truth I was a bit shocked and I thought it best if I just went and left you to it. I couldn't join in, there were only two people in the room that night and I wasn't one of them!"

"It won't make any difference to us, will it? Paul and I have agreed never to mention it again, it was rather a silly experiment that got out of hand."

"I don't know whether to be relieved or upset but it was a hell of an experience I won't forget in a hurry. We always agreed it wouldn't come between us and as far as I'm concerned it hasn't.

"Thanks Sal."

Izzie stood up, offered Sally another drink and gave her a hug. In late March they put their house up for rent and in April moved to a large apartment on the outskirts of Zurich. They wanted Sally to come out to see them in the autumn and she promised she would. Their leaving was very emotional, and Sally was aware that it would leave a huge gap in her life, but she was also aware that her life was about to change.

Easter was early and Maria went on holiday with her parents to the family home in Switzerland. She was away for two weeks and Sally felt bereft and lonely. This was becoming unnatural - or was it, pure boredom? She had plenty of friends and they would ask her out at weekends, but she still felt a certain awkwardness going out alone, she almost felt that they were asking her out as a sense of duty. She had made a great effort to be cheerful and back to her normal self although knew that as a result of her loss, things could never be the same again.

Maria resumed her lessons in mid April and Sally was so excited to see her it was, in her own mind, quite pathetic. They greeted with a kiss at the door, a continental equivalent of a handshake. Maria had brought her a bottle of Barolo and some Swiss chocolate.
"I know how you love your red wine and you look like you could do with a bit of chocolate".
This was the first time Maria had ever made mention of Sally's weight. It was true that since Dave had died she had lost a stone and although she didn't consider herself skinny, knew that she could put the stone back on without compromising her figure. They spent the next three hours discussing life, boyfriends, sex, parents, all in Spanish, as if they were sisters.
"Would you like to stay for lunch, I am only having a sandwich as I am going to the local pub tonight with my neighbours, but you are more than welcome".
Sally brought a plate of sandwiches into the dining room. Maria was looking at the box Sally's father had bought her.
"What a beautiful box, what is it?"
With that she opened the lid to reveal a row of cigars. Somewhat taken aback she said.
"You don't Smoke cigars do you?"

There was no point in lying. Sally told her that occasionally she smoked a cigar.

"But you are.....?"

"Are what?"

"So sensible, proper... old"

"And smoking the odd cigar isn't sensible and proper?"

Sally had never considered herself old and was stung by the accusation

"I didn't mean to offend; I just meant that you seemed normal"

"Let's eat!

Maria knew that her remarks hadn't been taken kindly and this was the first time there had been any sort of difficulty between them, trying to diffuse the situation she continued.

"My father has always smoked Swiss made 'Davidoffs', being the patriot he is, I love the smell but never considered smoking one myself, perhaps, I should try one?"

Maria had taken one from the box and was twisting it between her fingers. Perhaps it was the obvious phallic imagery or perhaps it was something else but Sally knew there was a feeling in her lower belly, almost like butterflies, there was something about this girl that did this to her, it was a feeling unlike any she ever had before, there was without doubt a sexual frisson, an atmosphere, surely Maria must feel it as well. She looked across the table at this young innocent girl; she had mixed emotions and almost felt 'dirty' at her own thoughts.

"When you pass with a grade 'A' we will open a bottle of Champagne and smoke one together, that's a promise."

Maria went home after lunch: Sally rang her neighbours and made an excuse, finished the bottle of Barolo and went to bed early. Radio 2 was her preferred listening; she and Dave went to bed very early on a Sunday as Dave had to be up at 4.30am to miss the traffic. She lay in bed and somehow couldn't get Maria out of her mind; this former student had somehow become a very important part of her life. It was wrong on virtually every level her thoughts were confused. Maria was 18, still at school, had a boyfriend, going to Cambridge; she was 40, her teacher and a widow, what on earth was going on? At least with Paul and Izzie they were all consenting adults, this girl was barely an adult!

Lying in bed in the darkness, her thoughts were of Maria, she pictured her in the shower. This was ludicrous, she had to get a grip, morally it was wrong, it was quite clearly a reaction to recent events, how could she possibly think of this girl in this way, she wasn't a lesbian, or at least she had never considered herself to be one, the brief physical contact with Izzie didn't mean she was – did it? She knew something, the feelings she had for this girl were not the same as those for Izzie, with Izzie it was a group thing, a ménage between three friends, this was somehow completely different. Her hand wandered ever so deliberately to her fanny and she delicately stroked her thick, dark hair, it didn't take long before she could feel her juices begin to flow, she stroked her lips and took her clitoris between her thumb and forefinger - this was so, so wrong!
    She woke at 6am with a start, it was very difficult to lie in after 15 years of routine. It's funny that guilt always seems worse in the dark, drinking her first cup of tea of the day she could somehow rationalise her emotions and knew that this was just a phase she was going through.

Maria took her exams in June she felt she had done ok but had to wait until August for the results. She had been accepted at Cambridge, subject to getting the required grades. As soon as her exams were over she went to the family home in Switzerland to spend the summer there with her boyfriend. Sally spent her summer mainly at home, enjoying her garden, going out with friends, eating in local pubs, basically just enjoying being without a care, she stilled missed Dave terribly though and barely a day went by when something or someone didn't remind her of happier times.

The phone rang and all Sally could hear was shouting, crying, laughing.

"Calm down and tell me"

"I got 3 'A's and its all down to you, I'm going to Cambridge, I'm so happy I just can't believe it. I am going out with my friends at lunchtime to celebrate, can I come around later."

"Of course you can, I already have a bottle of champagne on ice."

Sally was so excited for her success and was also excited knowing she was going to see her. It had been nearly six weeks since they had been together, and although she had filled her days it had been the longest six weeks of her life.

It was 4pm and Sally was mildly irritated, she thought that she would have been here by now, just then the phone rang, it was her mother.

"Hello, what do you want?"

"That's not a very nice greeting."

"I'm sorry, I was expecting another call, I didn't mean to be abrupt."

"Now it's nothing to worry about dear, but your father has had a mild heart attack, he's in hospital but they are going to send him home tomorrow."

"I'll come at the weekend to see him."

The door-bell rang.

"Sorry, someone's at the door I'll have to go, see you on Saturday, love to father."

With that she put down the phone and raced to the door. They embraced and hugged and kissed and just stood there on the doorstep, Sally not daring to move if it meant letting go. Maria was the first to speak.

"I'm ever so slightly tipsy, I'm afraid we got rather carried away, all the girls send their love and want to know if you are free a week on Friday, we would all like to take you out to the new wine bar in town, just to say 'thanks'."

Sally nodded; she was temporarily unable to speak. Suddenly without warning she started to cry.

"What's the matter?"

There was an awful lot the matter, she was pleased to see Maria, too pleased and she had been off hand with her mother at a time when she needed her. The problem was quite clearly the unnatural feelings for the girl standing in front of her, she only hoped it wasn't that obvious to Maria. She looked radiant, stunning, she had a deep tan from her recent holiday and had very little on, a beautiful white blouse that showed off her tan and one of the shortest skirts Sally had ever seen, she really did have magnificent legs.

"Nothing really, it's just that I have had some bad news about my father, but he's ok and it's not going to spoil our celebration tonight."

"How did you get here as you are obviously not driving?"

"Remember, Clare never touches a drop and was kind enough to give me a lift. Dad said he would pick me up later."

Sally had set up a couple of glasses and had put the bottle of champagne on ice. It was probably the hottest day of the year so far they certainly needed the shade of the big parasol as it would have been far too hot to sit in the direct sunlight. She poured two bubbling glasses of champagne and handed one to Maria.

"Here's to your success now and in the future."

It was another excuse for Sally to touch her, although this time she merely gave her a peck on the cheek.

"You must tell me all about your holiday, I've really missed you."

"I've missed you to, oh and before I forget I have brought you a couple of presents."

She reached down to her bag and gave Sally two nicely wrapped boxes. One was clearly a bottle of Wine the other, she assumed to be chocolates. On opening the small box she was astonished to see a box of Davidoffs.

"I thought if my father smoked them they must be ok, and by the way I tried a couple with my dad while we were in Switzerland, I thought we could share one later, you did promise you would if I got an 'A' and I know you like Barolo, apparently, according to my dad, a very good vintage."

They drank the bottle of champagne and Sally was feeling slightly light-headed, she also realised Maria was talking in a more animated and open style.

"If you don't mind I need to ring my mother. Open the second bottle and help yourself; I won't be long."

"You don't mind if I take a shower do you, but it was dreadfully hot and sticky in town."

"No, of course not, take as long as you like."

Sally still felt guilty from the previous conversation with her mother and wanted to assuage her feelings and find out how her father was. He was 'quite perky', according to her mother and was sitting up in his hospital bed ordering around the nurses.

"Should be home tomorrow darling, I am absolutely dreading it, you would have thought they would have kept him in a little bit longer."

Sally could hear the shower running and had a mental picture, her mother continued as she always did, basically about trivia and what the neighbours were up to. The shower stopped and she heard the door open.

"I have to go, mum, (she very rarely called her 'mum', her parents preferred 'mummy' and 'daddy' but when she reached 40 she decided it was rather childish), I have a guest and I am beginning to neglect her, see you on Saturday."

She heard Maria walking down the stairs.

"Sorry to be a nuisance but I haven't got a towel."

Sally opened the door fully and there in front of her, standing very naked was Maria, her long hair was cascading over her shoulders, small trickles of water running over her dark brown breasts, her nipples, even darker, the only white mark was a small triangle around her very, very, smooth mound, gone was the thick black hair that Sally remembered so well from the previous summer. She couldn't take her eyes from this vision of loveliness.

"Towel?"

"Sorry, of course."

"Don't worry, if you haven't a clean one, I'll dry off outside."

"No, no, I'll fetch you one."

"Might as well go outside anyway as I'm downstairs now."

With that she brushed past Sally and disappeared through the French Windows. Sally watched her go; she was almost breathless with excitement. She stood there not daring to think, not daring to move, in case she would suddenly awake from this dream, this was not happening, this wasn't real, she was a young girl again in the flush of youth - what was happening to her?

Sally hesitated at the door not quite knowing what to do. Her stomach was in total turmoil, she picked up the towel and took it outside. Maria was lying on the hammock and made a move to get up.

"Stay there, I will sit on the lounger."

Maria stood up, totally unabashed, totally uninhibited, totally young and nubile, totally gorgeous, totally nude. Facing Sally, she wrapped the towel around her.

"Thanks", she said, as though she had just taken a glass of wine from her.

"If you open the other bottle I'll go and light one of your dad's favourite Davidoff's, after all it's not every day someone wins a place at Cambridge."

Sally went upstairs, quickly showered and changed into what she referred to as her 'leisure gear', she had a pair of very light cotton pantaloons Dave had brought back from the Far East and one of Dave's cotton open neck shirts. She dispensed of her underwear as she liked the feel of the soft, loose cotton next to her body and wearing the shirt reminded her of happier times. She looked at herself in the full-length mirror and was pleased with what she saw; her body was good for a 40 year old, she had put back the stone she had lost and it suited her. There was, at a certain angle and in a certain light the unmistakeable dark shadow at the top of her legs and if she looked closely enough could see the outline of her breasts and her now, very stiff nipples, but considering what she had just witnessed, felt she might have even been overdressed. She carefully lit one of her new Swiss cigars, they were slightly shorter, but slightly fatter than her own brand and she was surprised how mild they tasted.

"Would you mind if I stayed the night as I'm not sure I want my dad to see me like this?"

"Of course, you can, you can even choose your bedroom."

Sally took a sip of her champagne and passed the cigar to Maria who, to Sally's total surprise, took a deep puff and after a second or two blew out three perfect smoke rings from the 'o' her perfectly formed lips made.

"So, where did you learn to do that?"

I told you I had been practising with my dad, I'm still not sure whether I like the taste but it just seems a totally relaxing thing to do."

For the next hour they drank, smoked whilst sharing confidences, gone was the need to speak in another tongue, liberal amounts of alcohol compensated for that.

"I think of you as an older sister."

Sally wasn't sure if this was a good connection or not but enjoyed the closeness, nonetheless. They were both now inebriated and, as the champagne flowed, so did the conversation.

"When I was in Switzerland I let my boyfriend shave me, it was the most sensuous and erotic thing I have ever done."

Sally didn't know what to say, she wasn't certain whether she preferred the new look, it was definitely different, she made no mention of the fact that she had noticed as she didn't want to seem too interested.

"Dave liked me the way I was – hairy, a hairy fanny and hairy underarms."

Sally was surprised at her own frank language.

"Seriously Sally you should try it, I can't believe how nice it makes me feel, my boyfriend can't get enough. It has made a complete difference to our relationship. I was in Switzerland for nearly six weeks and apart from a few days in the middle we had sex every day and sometimes twice a day."

Sally had never had sex every day for six weeks and rarely twice in one day. She was certain however; no-one, was ever going to shave her pussy!

They began to talk nonsense and knew they were drunk. Sally smoked another Davidoff and opened the bottle of Barolo. The night was warm and fine and about 10pm a full moon appeared, it lit the patio and was as bright as the dullest winter's day. There conversation became stilted and they both realised that they were quite, quite, drunk.

"It's no good Maria I'm going to bed I'll show you to your room."

They kissed lightly on the cheek and said goodnight. Sally went to her bedroom and without putting on the light took off her clothes and lay on top of her bed. The light of the full moon lit the bedroom and she could clearly see her outline. She was frustrated by the night's events and although she had enjoyed the company it had left her with an aching, that in her mind was both unnatural and morally wrong, nevertheless it was certainly real and was beginning to eat away at her. She lay there and as she closed her eyes, the room spun, she was even too tired to consider playing with herself.

She didn't know how long she had been asleep or what time it was but felt someone slip into bed next to her. Suddenly any tiredness disappeared. Almost instantaneously she felt moist lips touch hers with lightness at first and then, with ever increasing passion, felt a tongue gently feel hers. They kissed for what seemed an age, each exploring the others lips and soft palate, exchanging the remnants of champagne, red wine, cigar smoke. Maria lowered her head and started to tease and tickle Sally's very erect nipples, expertly moving her tongue in a circular motion around each tip and at the same time massaging each breast with her hands. Up to now Sally had been subordinate: she was now fully awake and reached down with her left hand and felt for the very first time, the ripeness, smoothness, wetness of the other's beautifully shaved cunt, she couldn't believe how good it felt, after years of touching her own very hairy one, this was something very different. Maria moved her body into a position that enabled Sally to easily explore every part of her womanhood and as she did Sally could hear Maria's breathing change. She couldn't believe how soft and wet she was, she used one finger and then two and thrust in time with Maria's breathing which was now becoming shallow and quick, the more she thrust the louder the breathing, until suddenly there was almost a shout as she came, almost crushing Sally's fingers as her vaginal muscles spasmed.

They lay there in silence, no-one spoke, it wasn't embarrassment it was recognition of what they had just done. It seemed an age and then Sally felt Maria's hair on her stomach and felt her soft lips kiss her breasts, then very slowly felt her working her way down as if she was drawing patterns with her tongue, she seemed to spend a long time delicately touching the very top of her pubes as though she was testing what was underneath: suddenly without warning her mouth went straight to her opening and Sally sensed her clitoris being squeezed between teeth, for a brief second there was a sharp pain that made her moan but almost immediately this was replaced by a most delicious feeling. For the next twenty minutes or so Maria kissed, sucked, licked, nibbled, tugged every part of Sally's cunt, not content with that she then moved her own into a sixty-nine position so Sally could do the same to her. Sally sunk her head deep into Maria and French kissed her lovely mound, exchanging her saliva with Maria's now gorgeous wetness, it was as if she was kissing her face: she placed her lips on her and with her tongue explored every part, inside and out, she loved her smell, in fact she loved every bit of her.

They had sex once more that night, a far less intense affair than the first two times.

Sally knelt astride Maria and started to massage her, she had done this to Dave many times in their marriage and considered herself to be some sort of expert: starting with her tender slim neck she made her way down her body, lightly kneading her flesh, playing with her nipples before continuing her journey: this time she merely massaged the surface of her fanny taking care not to enter her. After fifteen minutes or so she asked Maria to turn over and began the same process on her back: when she got to her lower back Sally turned around and was facing the end of the bed, her strong hands, from years of playing sport, working on Maria's buttocks, it was without doubt the loveliest bottom she had ever seen. She started very slowly at first but with each massage she deliberately forced the cheeks apart until eventually slipping her left hand between her crack. She touched the velvety rosebud beneath her finger and for a moment she felt Maria stiffen but almost instantaneously she relaxed and let Sally continue. Sally's hand slid up and down stopping at her moist, but not now wet vagina while at the same time she started to ride up and down; her own bush, wet on Maria's back, massaging her own lips as she did so. Their movements were as one, Sally's fingers sliding between Maria's two damp holes as Maria moved in time with Sally's riding motion. Maria was the first to come although it was a much more muted affair than the two previous occasions. Sally ignored Maria and with both hands now free, looked to her own selfish needs. Eventually too much alcohol and tiredness took over and Sally lay down next to her, wrapping her right arm and right leg over Maria's now sleeping body, in a warm embrace.

Sally was the first to wake; she opened her eyes and was confronted with the sight of Maria a mere six inches away. She stared at her, looking at her loveliness, she guessed that this would be the last time she would see her like this and wanted to remember how it was. She quietly got out of bed so as not to disturb her, she pulled the quilt up from the bottom of the bed where they had left it the night before and gently covered Maria's still, sleeping body. She had a long hot shower, washing last night's debris from her body and went downstairs, she had a bad headache and her mouth felt, to use an old cliché, like the bottom of a parrot's cage. She made herself tea. While she was drinking her second cup the door of the kitchen opened and Maria stood there in Sally's dressing gown.

"I've been lying there thinking of what to say, I was too embarrassed to come down"

"Don't say anything, there's nothing to say and nothing to feel guilty about. You have a nice boyfriend, you're off to Cambridge and you had a lovely day yesterday and got slightly drunk - that's it!"

"There's not a cup of tea going is there, I feel pretty rough."

Sally stood up, went across to Maria and kissed her very tenderly on the lips, there was no sexual intent, given or taken. They held hands and looked into each other's eyes, both knowing they were about to go their separate ways.

CHAPTER 5

THE 'CAMP' CAMPER VAN!

She walked the three miles to town it would be dark when she came back and would take a taxi. The wine bar had only been open for a few months and was still in its honeymoon period. She had to push past the smokers and drinkers hanging outside, 'God', how she hated the smell of cigarette smoke. It was full of beautiful young girls, wearing very little and seemingly all with deep tans. As a result, it was also full of 20,30,40 something men, having a drink on the way home from work. The noise was incredible, music blaring away, although barely discernible over the general chatter and laughter.

Clare was the first to greet her, she stood there with a glass of orange in her hand looking lonely and was very pleased to see Sally. They kissed on the cheek, before they had time to say anything they were joined by four of her other 'girls' who had arrived in the same taxi.
"What would you like to drink Sally?"
"A glass of merlot would be nice but let me get it."
"No, this is our celebration, this is a thank you from all of us."
The girl who spoke was Charlotte, she was the leader of the pack, always the one with the first and last word. She was popular with the others, tall, attractive, clever, sporty, the complete package. Sally looked at them, not sure whether she really did have lesbian thoughts. Surely, she couldn't have turned from a heterosexual 40 year old into a dyke almost overnight?
"Where's Maria?"
"Didn't she text you, she can't make it, something to do with a family matter."

It hit her like a steam train, suddenly she realised how much she had been looking forward to seeing Maria. It had been over a week and she hadn't had a text or an email.

"No, but I don't always look at my texts and I have left my phone at home."

She was trying to hide her obvious disappointment from the others and wondered if anyone had noticed anything amiss in her manner.

"She did say that there was a possibility if she finished early she would come later."

This news cheered Sally somewhat. The girls were very happy, all of them had got into their university of choice and they couldn't stop talking, laughing, discussing their future plans. They did their best to include Sally but tonight she was an outsider.

At about 10pm Sally said she thought she ought to be going and organised a taxi. The taxi arrived a few minutes later and as she walked towards the door she saw Maria arrive: they met in the entrance, neither knowing what to say, it was Maria who spoke first.

"You're not going as soon as I arrive are you?"

"I didn't think you were coming, you didn't let me know."

"I did, I sent you an email yesterday."

Sally had religiously looked at her emails every day since Maria had left that morning a week ago, yesterday she hadn't bothered as she expected she would be seeing her."

Maria kissed her on both cheeks: it was as a friend, not a lover.

"I have to go, you don't need me here, go and see your friends. Let me know how you get on in Cambridge and do send me the odd email, I'd like to keep in touch with you all."

She knew she had to go. What had happened could and should never be repeated, it had clearly suited them both albeit for totally different reasons. She thought she saw a tear in Maria's eye, they kissed once more and Sally got into her taxi and went home.

As soon as she got home she turned on her computer to look at her email. There were quite a few unopened but the one she was searching for was from Maria, it was of course there, just as Maria said it would be. She opened it.

Hi Sally

Sorry haven't been in touch, but my Mum took me shopping to London for the weekend, a sort of celebration for getting into Cambridge and she bought me a load of things for Uni. Then on Tuesday my Dad got a call from my uncle in Switzerland to say Grandma was very ill and in hospital. We all flew out yesterday and I don't expect to be back in time to meet you all at the wine bar as my flight doesn't get in until 6pm at Gatwick tomorrow, I'll try my best as I would like to see all the girls again and you of course.

Thanks for everything and if I don't see you before I go off to Cambridge I will email you and let you know how I'm getting on.

Love Maria x

She knew in that one email that there would never be another time: she had to think of it as part of her rehabilitation. She scanned down and could see she that Izzie had written, she always loved to read emails from her friend and opened it.

Sal

Well we're back from our 3 week holiday, everybody seems to take a month over here, anyway we only got back a couple of days ago. You can't imagine how much washing I've got to do, the boys do nothing but fight and we are looking for a bigger flat I can't wait for the boys to go back to boarding school. It looks like Paul is going to be here much longer than we thought, well at least for 3 years anyway. I can't wait to see you at the end of

September I know we get together at least once a month when I come home to see my dad but I really miss you. I've got loads of things organised for us to do unfortunately Paul will be working I say unfortunately but I'm sure he'd only get in the way.

Sally had realised since she'd been receiving regular emails from Izzie, that she wrote as she spoke, at a hundred miles an hour, very little punctuation and rambling sentences, but she liked the style as she could almost hear her friend speaking to her.

Ring me Sal and let me know what you've been up to while we've been away I'm dying to catch up. Leave it until the end of next week as the boys go to their grandparents for a few days next Wednesday then thank God they go back to school in a couple of weeks.
  Love Izzie xxxx

Sally knew that there were certain things she could tell her, but one thing was for certain, she wouldn't be mentioning Maria!

She scrolled down, there were a couple of emails she didn't recognise and wondered why her spam filter hadn't dealt with them, she then spotted one from an old friend, Karen, it was her best friend from University and they had been inseparable since the first day at Sheffield. Karen was everything Sally wasn't, she was outward going and forthright, outrageous in her behaviour, slept with lots of boys but never loved any of them, would wander naked around their flat that they shared, drank like a fish but never, never got a hangover, never had a mood although occasionally aggressive, but she was like a sister to Sally and her best friend. They had kept in touch for quite a few years and she had stayed with Sally and Dave on many occasions. Quite a few years after Sally married, Karen had introduced her Spanish boy friend to them and for some reason both Dave and Sally had taken an instant dislike to him. The evening was not a success, they tried again but it was even worse, they thought he was a user and didn't like the way he treated Karen and after that they just seemed to drift apart, as friends do sometimes. Sally had heard from another mutual university friend that Karen had married him and had moved to Spain, she was apparently teaching English at a high school.

Hello Sally

Thought I would write to you, I've been meaning to write for ages. I recently heard about Dave from one of our old University friends and I'm so sorry, I really liked him, you must have been through hell and back, she also told me that you've given up work. I've had a few traumas myself, although nothing like yours. I guess you and Dave and a lot of my other friends were right about Miguel, it's a pity it took over ten years to see him for what he was. He left me at the beginning of the year.

I was so sad that me and you drifted apart, you were my best friend at University and I have missed you so much. I wanted to write, but I knew you and Dave couldn't stand Miguel so there seemed little point, anyway you could have written to me as well: that sounded a bit shitty – sorry, you know what I'm like.

Sally did and thought the last remark was typically Karen, she missed her forthrightness.

Anyway, I am on my own and have taken a sabbatical for a year to get my head together. I have a lovely apartment in Alicante overlooking the sea, courtesy of Miguel, he might have been a complete bastard but he knew how to make money. Come on Sally, how about flying out for a few days, if we don't get on it won't be the end of the world. I'll pick you up from the airport and we'll go out on the town! I don't suppose you're still very good at it and I haven't done it for ten years, but it will be like old times.

Please email me back, even if it's a 'no'.
Love and kisses
Karen xx

Sally made herself a drink, put on Grieg's piano concerto in A minor on the cd and sat down on her favourite chair. It was now the end of August she had enjoyed the summer, but winter was looming and she needed to decide what she was going to do. She could go and see her friends although she needed a purpose, she couldn't go through a winter at home with nothing to do, she knew she would get depressed and bored.

It came to her in the early hours of the morning, she had been lying awake all night tossing and turning, thinking of what she was going to do when she had a totally mad idea. She would buy a small camper van and travel around Europe. In her early years when her father was trying to build his business they had very little money and they used to tow a caravan all over France and Spain for their holidays, it was this that gave her the love she had for language and different cultures. She would start by driving to Switzerland and then go to Spain: that was the first two weeks sorted out. She decided there and then that as soon as she got up, she would ring her father, he would sort out a good van for her as she knew nothing about them.

At 9 am the next morning, a Saturday, Sally rang her parents.

"Daddy I need to speak to you about buying a vehicle."

"What sort of vehicle?"

"A camper van."

"A camper van – why?"

She told him her plan.

"What are you doing today? Why don't you come over for lunch and I'll take you down to my garage? They sell cars but they are part of a big group and I know Mercedes sell those sorts of things."

"O.K., it's just after 9, I will be with you about 12.

When she arrived her father had already been on the phone to his garage and they had arranged for Sally and her father to go to another garage in the group that specialised in vans and camper vans.

"We've time for a quick coffee and then I'll drive you over, it's on the outskirts but it will only take us half an hour on a Saturday, I told them we'd be there about 1.30. By the way mummy is coming if that's o.k?"

"Of course it is, where is she?"

"She's doing a bit of shopping, but she said she would be back about 12.30. She thinks you may have lost your marbles and really can't understand why a single woman wants to roam around Europe in a van."

"What do you think?"

Before he could answer her mother arrived home. She kissed Sally and immediately asked her what she was thinking about. Seeing the look on Sally's face her father interjected.

"Well I think it's a brilliant idea, you have no ties, you're still young and it's not even that you can't speak the language. If I was twenty years younger, I'd go."

"It would be without me!"

"I wish you'd told me that before."

They all smiled as they all knew categorically that would never have happened, he might have seemed to have 'worn the trousers', but anyone who knew them really well, knew that her mother was the real 'power behind the throne'.

When they arrived at the garage the salesman was waiting for them, clearly he had been told to look after them as Sally's father had been a very important customer of the group for over twenty years, always insisting that his fleet of vehicles in his business were Mercedes. There were about thirty different vans to choose from, Sally couldn't believe how luxurious they were on the inside, she certainly could see a big difference from the caravans she used to stay in as a child.

"If we start with the size, we can narrow the search down."

"I will probably be on my own most of the time, but if I am going away for a long time I don't want a really small one, I want one I can spread about in and I don't want to have to make a bed up every night."

"In that case a four berth would probably suit you best."

They looked at the first couple he showed them although they didn't do anything for her, after another three or four she was beginning to think she wouldn't find anything suitable.

"The salesman was starting to think that it wasn't his day."

"Haven't you got anything else."

"The only other one of this size is in the workshop, it only came in this morning, I don't know what state it's in. It was owned by a couple of........" he hesitated for a moment before continuing "....a couple of gentlemen."

"Let's go and look at it then."

It was immaculate, it had been custom made to their requirements, there were two single beds very close together, there was a living area with built in everything, satellite t.v., music pod, the kitchenette was beautifully compact and incredibly equipped, finally the shower area had been customised and there wasn't just one shower head but five different attachments, some with very interesting shapes. The walls had been hand-painted and it was with erotic art, although modern in style, there could be no doubt as to what some of the objects were. This undoubtedly was the one she wanted.

"How much is this one?"

"I'm sorry because it only came in today it's not yet on the system."

Her father could see the glint in Sally's eye, unfortunately it was matched by the very large glint in the salesman's eye.

"I tell you what, we need to go now, but here's my number, if you could give me a ring later this afternoon and give some indication of the price, I would appreciate it."

Sally knew what was happening and didn't try to say anything, she knew that her father was in business mode and knew he would get a much better deal than she ever could.

When they arrived home the garage had already rang.

"They are very keen, I don't think we will ring just yet."

Sally didn't argue, she knew he wanted to do the best deal he could, she also knew how helpless he had felt when Dave died and doing this small task somehow made up for it. She wouldn't get involved even if it meant losing the van. They had a splendid lunch, as always, but Sally's father could sense that she was agitated.

"I'll give them a call as they will be closing in half an hour. Sally are you certain this is the one for you, we can go and look at other garages tomorrow and you haven't said what your budget is."

"I don't want to pay more than £35,000."

"£35,000, have you got that sort of money?"

She didn't answer; instead she helped her mother clear the table while her father picked up the phone and rang the salesman. From the kitchen Sally could hear her them talking but not what he was saying, after a few minutes he came into the room.

"You can pick it up on Wednesday, they need to service and tax it and it's yours for £32,750, are you sure it's what you want?"

"Me and mummy will drive over Wednesday morning and pick you up."

As she drove it along the M4 she felt empowered, sexy almost, whether it was the seating position, higher than most cars and 4 x 4's or whether it was the feeling of just driving something large, she didn't know, she did know that this was going to become her home for the next, however long and she was totally excited at the prospect. She arrived home just as it was getting dark and parked it in her drive, it dwarfed her mini, they looked in her mind like a mother and daughter. She locked it up and went inside, she had a couple of emails to write.

Evening Izzie

You'll never guess what I've done? I've bought a camper van, it's brilliant, a couple of old gays used to own it and they drove it around Europe on a grand tour for two years until unfortunately one of them died; it was what they had always promised each other, a bit sad really, but it's absolutely beautiful and you just won't believe the shower unit, totally hand painted with erotic art.

Anyway, I have decided to do exactly the same, starting with my trip to see you at the end of September then going to see Karen an old University friend who lives in Spain.

I'll call you tomorrow and tell you more, but I am going to email Karen now and give her the news.

Love, Sally x

Hi Karen

Just picked up your email (she lied) *it's great to hear from you I've often thought about you and 'yes' I would love to come and see you. I have spent the last eighteen months 'licking my wounds', although you might be a bit surprised as I have become a bit of a changed person, I seem to have got rid of some of my inhibitions you always told me I had. Anyway, I have just bought myself a camper van and intend to tour Europe, I am driving to Switzerland the last week in September to see Izzie and Paul, you met them briefly with me and Dave, but I don't suppose you remember, whatever, I plan to drive down and be with you*

the first Saturday in October. Don't worry, if we don't get on I can always clear off in my van.
Let me know if that suits?
Love, Sally x

Sally went outside and looked at her new purchase, she couldn't wait for the morning to have a proper look. She went back inside, opened a bottle of champagne, sat in her armchair and toasted herself. She thought she ought to give her van a name, she would, she decided, sleep on it. This was the start of a new chapter, although looking back who would have thought that since Dave had died, she had been seduced by an 18 year old student and her best friends (twice). Neither had been of her doing, or had they? One thing was for certain she hadn't been an unwilling partner and had basically enjoyed every minute of it, even though she still had some difficulty with the last episode with Paul and Izzie. She just couldn't help thinking about Paul's big fat knob, she finished her glass of champagne, poured herself another glass and knew she had to go and find 'Paul'. Slipping her knickers down she introduced him to her moist opening and with a bit of difficulty forced him into her: she wasn't quite wet enough, but there was no hurry, took another drink and carefully moved him up and down, occasionally taking 'him' out and rubbing him between her lips: with her eyes closed she pictured the real thing, what would Dave have thought? She knew though, that it was a perfect end to a perfect day.

The next morning at 7 before her mandatory cup of tea she went outside and unlocked her van. She loved it, especially the shower and could picture herself in some foreign land showering herself after a tiring day on the beach. She knew she had made the right decision although before driving on the continent she needed to try it out nearer home. There were lots of camp sites only a few miles radius from her home on the edge of the New Forest and the wonderful Dorset coast. She would go on the net and find somewhere to try it out this coming weekend. Turning on her computer she was surprised that she had already had a reply from Karen.

Sally

I can't wait to see you: the first weekend in October is perfect. My God you have changed, who would have thought that you would contemplate driving a camper van all over Europe, you will be telling me next, that you run around naked and shag everything in sight.

I'll organise a bit of an itinerary, Benidorm isn't too far and is always great for a wild couple of days and I know a great beach just up the coast, we could park on the campsite next to it and just chill out. The weather should still be really warm. Sorry Sally, here I go again, I was always trying to organise you when we were at University together, although I never succeeded in the 'shagging department' for you.

Forget all that I just got carried away, have a think about what you want to do, email me back and I'll give you a call, presumably your phone number is the same.

Love and kisses
Karen xx

It was just like old times this was the sort of conversation she would have had with her nearly twenty years before. She trawled the net and found a small campsite about fifteen miles away she rang the number and wasn't too surprised to hear that they had plenty of reservations; it was almost the end of the holiday season. She booked in from Saturday until the following Tuesday, that gave her three nights, she considered that would be long enough to get a feel for it. One way or another it was going to be an adventure!

She arrived on the site at lunchtime Saturday, it was a small site set within the heart of the New Forest, there were a few problems she knew she had to overcome and not the least was the erection of the awning. An hour's instruction on the workings of the van was probably not enough to equip her and certainly didn't make her an expert, however, on a quiet site, on a pitch away from anybody else was the place to learn. She was surprised that when she arrived it was a lot busier than she had imagined, it didn't look anything like the pictures on the net and for an instant she believed that she may have been on the wrong site, however, she recognised the reception from the pictures she'd seen. She was given a site with no near neighbours, it was perfect, it was private with a great back drop of the New Forest. She drove to the site and carefully parked, even though there were no immediate neighbours she imagined that there would be many eyes on her, she decided that once she had connected the services she would make a cup of tea before attempting to erect the awning. It was a lovely autumn day and sipping her tea in the afternoon sunshine she took stock of her surroundings. There was a mix of caravans and camper vans, mainly the former but one particular camper van stood out from the rest. It was at least half as long again as hers, she wondered what sort of people would own such a vehicle. She finished her tea and decided to erect the awning, it looked very simple when the salesman showed her but with it laid out on the ground it seemed a daunting task.

"Hello."

She looked up and saw an elderly couple looking at her.

"Can we help?"

"You're new to this aren't you?"

It was obvious, she couldn't deny it.

"A bit."

"When we saw you arrive we guessed you hadn't done this sort of thing before."

"How did you know?"

"You just get a hunch, we've been doing this all our life, it's the little things like parking and choosing your pitch. The one you've picked will only get the sun first thing in the morning and the trees will make a terrible mess of your van."

"Oh."

Sally couldn't think of anything to say.

"We'll put up your awning and you just watch, by the way I'm Bryan and this is my wife Janet."

Sally wasn't sure that she wanted this intrusion, but she knew that without their help it was unlikely she would put up the awning before dark and even then she had her doubts.

Ten minutes later and with military precision the awning was up and looking splendid.

"Would you like a cup of tea that's the least I can do…..or perhaps a glass of wine?"

"It's a little bit early for us, isn't it, Janet?"

Up to this point Janet hadn't really uttered a word.

"I don't think so Bryan, the sun is well and truly over the yard arm."

They both sniggered at the old cliché.

"Red or white?"

"White would be good."

Sally disappeared into the van and brought out a bottle and three glasses.

"Where's Bryan?"

"He's gone to fetch a couple of chairs."

She saw him heading for the splendid van she had seen when she had arrived. So, they're the sort of people who own such a fantastic van. A few moments later Bryan arrived with two magnificent chairs, they wouldn't have been out of place in Sally's lounge. Sally poured three large glasses and emptied the bottle.

"I'll be rather tipsy if I drink all that."

Janet was looking rather anxiously at her husband as if seeking his permission.

"Better stick to one old girl we don't want you getting drunk, do we?"

Sally thought the remark was rather condescending, but Janet brushed it aside, obviously used to it. For a few moments they drank in silence and Sally was beginning to feel rather uncomfortable. She looked at her watch and realised she had only been on the site for about an hour and already the peace and solitude she'd hoped for had been shattered, however, she wasn't sorry as she realised that she was on a very steep learning curve and any help she could get was welcome.

"We've been caravanning for forty years we have four kids and it was the only way we could afford to have a holiday. They are all grown up now, so when the last one left home we decided to take early retirement and buy a camper van. We have been all over Europe, haven't we dear?"

The question was not meant to have an answer, nor did it; Janet just looked at her husband and smiled. The next half an hour went by very quickly, in that time Sally learnt all about them without ever having to talk about herself. Bryan was a retired local government officer and Janet was a retired primary school teacher and they had both taken early retirement and were clearly enjoying their life.

"Come on Janet drink up I'm sure Sally has a lot to do."

Sally was quite relieved at their sudden departure.

"We're having a barbeque tonight, fancy popping over?"

She didn't, but she hadn't anything else to do and they seemed decent enough people.

"Um."

"Go on we can at least repay your hospitality."

By the time Sally arrived it was already dark, and she could see the glow of the barbeque and their shadowy figures.

"You needn't have brought us another bottle we have plenty of stock, Janet sees to that, don't you dear?"

Sally thought that Bryan just might get on her nerves after a time, but if Janet didn't seem to mind his slightly patronising tone then why should she? Bryan was very clearly in charge of the barbeque, 'the typical man thing', Sally thought, the only cooking Dave ever did was 'al fresco', there was just something about men and fires, it probably went back to the psychi of the caveman.

"What would you like to drink, G and T, red, white?"

"G and T would be rather nice."

Sally sat down in a very luxurious armchair, these two seemed to have everything to hand and every bit of equipment one could possibly want. As the drink flowed, Janet became more talkative and the relationship between her and her husband seemed to change, he, more relaxed, she, funny, clever, erudite. It turned out that she had been to Oxford, had a degree in English Literature and then almost at once after gaining her degree, married Bryan and had two boys and two girls. Only when the children reached their teenage years did she go back to college and take a teaching diploma.

"Quite honestly dear, I didn't fancy dealing with other people's teenagers if mine were typical and I thought I was past it, so primary school was enough, and I had a simply lovely career. I ended up as a headmistress but when everything started to change I realised that I was just doing the work of a secretary and HR manager and when Bryan was offered early retirement we decided to 'go for it', and we are having an absolute ball!"

She looked at her husband who nodded in agreement. There had been a complete juxtaposition of the relationship from the afternoon: to Sally they had probably both worked out what each did well and played to each other's strengths, a recipe for a good marriage, similar to her own parents.

Dinner was an absolutely brilliant feast, Sally couldn't believe what Bryan had produced on a barbeque. They sat in the awning as it was quite cold outside, but the table was resplendent with a white tablecloth, a candelabra and a sort of outside gas log fire, it was beautifully warm and she felt very at home in this tent, perhaps she could get hers as nice. They asked Sally about her life and sympathised with her recent loss, there was no doubt she was warming to this couple and by the end of the night she felt she had known them for years.

"So, Sally what are your future plans?"

She told them of her intended travels to Switzerland and Spain and then, wherever 'the van' took her.

"We are going down to one of our favourite sites at the end of September for a month, we go every year, it's a fantastic naturist friendly, privately wooded site, why don't you come and stay on your way to your friend in Alicante, Janet and I can show you the ropes."

Sally was feeling very relaxed, very full of drink and wine and in a way it sounded quite a good plan. She had her own van it wasn't like she would be living with them and any help would be welcome as she still didn't feel very capable of erecting her awning. It would be great to get back to nature and in her 'mind's eye' she could picture the site with a few birds, squirrels running around and in her relaxed state, it sounded like heaven.

"So, will you come for a few days?"

The two of them exchanged glances and then looked at Sally.

"Brilliant, of course I will."

"Great, I will email you the details; just let us know when, to fit in with your plans."

Sally said her goodbyes, stumbled back to her van, fell into bed and didn't remember anything until the next morning.

When she woke, she could hear the rain splashing on her van roof, she had a thumping head and felt a little nauseous. She slowly remembered the previous evening and with ever rising panic recalled that she had agreed to meet Janet and Bryan on a site on the Costa something or other in about three weeks. She made her mandatory tea and went back to bed to drink it, after washing a couple of painkillers down she started to gradually feel a little better. It was ten thirty before she could face the world and for the first time, tried out the *erotic* shower, although nothing, but nothing could be further than her thoughts. She stood in the steaming hot water and let the refreshing streams of water cascade down her body; looking down at herself she decided that since leaving school and playing very little sport her body was beginning to look its age, which was one of the reasons she had bought herself a bike. First things first though she needed to renew her acquaintance with her 'new' friends and find out exactly what she had agreed to.

"Fancy a coffee?"

The pair of them looked ridiculously healthy, she realised that in spite of their previous protestations to the contrary, they probably drank more than she did.

"I don't want to put you to any trouble I just came to say thanks for last night."

"Don't be silly we always have a pot of coffee on the go."

'Of course, they f……. did,' Sally thought and could now smell the delicious brew emanating from the open doorway.

"You haven't seen our van properly have you, come on in and I'll show you around."

Janet guided her into the main sitting room, it was, Sally thought, without doubt, although she was no expert, the most beautiful camper van on the planet. She was quite plainly in awe of this beauty. As Janet showed her around she probably guessed Sally's reaction and as if to justify it somehow, she said.

"We downsized when we retired and sold our large house and moved into a smaller one, with the money we made we invested in this as we thought we might be spending more time in this than the house."

"It's absolutely fantastic, gorgeous, brilliant - I love it."

She couldn't really think of anything else to say and would be in danger of running out of superlatives if she didn't stop.

The news didn't seem too bad, apparently, she had agreed to meet them a few days before meeting up with Karen. The campsite was well known to Bryan and Janet, they had been there for five years running and was at the northern end of the Costa Dorada, set amongst pine scented hills with direct access to the beach, it sounded idyllic. It was still about 400 miles from Alicante, but it would nicely break the journey. Sally was just beginning to realise what a huge journey she was undertaking.

"We didn't think you would come after you had a chance to sleep on it, did we Janet? I'm sure you will love the life after trying it a few times, have you ever been to these type of sites before?"

Sally wasn't exactly certain what they meant by 'these type of sites'; she assumed they were referring to Spanish camp and caravan sites.

"My parents used to take me when I was young; we went mainly to the west coast of France though, as my father didn't like towing the caravan too far."

"So, you never went with your husband?"

"No, Dave and I liked 5 star hotels."

"I'll send you detailed instructions on how to get there, when do you think you'll come?"

Janet went inside again and brought out a calendar, they were clearly not taking 'no' for an answer. It was decided that she would arrive on Monday the 29th September and leave on Friday the 3rd October this would give her 2 full days to travel from Zurich as she wanted to spend one night on the Riviera and would give her the best part of 2 days to travel down to Alicante as long as she got an early start on the Friday.

"That's settled then, do you want me to book it for you?"

Sally nodded, believing it would be easy to cancel if she changed her mind. The pair of them seemed totally delighted and even though to use Janet's words, 'the sun wasn't quite over the yard arm', they insisted on opening a bottle of sparkling wine. Sally's stomach recoiled at the thought of yet more alcohol so early but being the well brought up girl she was and seeing the look on their faces she agreed to one glass.

It wasn't overly warm but good bike riding weather and Sally needed to get some exercise and clear her head. She had planned a route of about 20 miles that took her through the most beautiful part of the New Forest. She found the first few miles quite tiring as it was mainly in an upwards direction and after an hour she was pleased to stop at the first pub she saw. It was about 2pm and she realised that she was quite hungry, she ordered a sandwich and a Perrier water, she needed to take on water after the previous night's excesses and her late morning wine. Sitting outside in the autumn sunshine she reflected on the previous twenty months or so and wasn't quite sure what she had turned into, she was certainly aware of one thing, Dave wouldn't have recognised her new found sexual freedom, she wasn't even sure if she did: at least her new friends Bryan and Janet didn't pose a threat in that direction.

The last couple of miles seemed to take ages and she couldn't wait to have a shower, sit down in her awning with a large glass of merlot, that was something else she noticed, barely a day went past without an alcoholic drink although, 'sod it' she would also have a cigar, it would be the first one she had ever had on a caravan site and anyway it was no-one's business other then hers. Her body ached, especially her muscles around the top of her legs where the saddle had rubbed against her, her back felt cold where the sweat had now dried, although still leaving her jumper damp. She slipped off her clothes and walked into the shower. It wasn't a large cubicle and definitely couldn't have accommodated two people but was adequate for her needs. She stood there for a full ten minutes letting her body soak up the water, it was almost as if her body was taking in the water and re-hydrating her. The erotica was there although it was difficult to see through the steam and as she soaped her body she reached for the phallic head and started to rub it against her. She could only have imagined where in the past it might have been, but however revolting the thought that may have been two years before, it wasn't now. Gently rubbing her clitoris she could feel the water spraying all around her, it was as though there was an unseen hand massaging her outer parts and she knew she was wet inside. She slightly bent her knees to position herself and then very gently introduced the shower head between her lips, it was the most incredible feeling she had ever had, it felt this time that not one hand was at work, but many, almost at once before she even had a chance to push it into her, she came. It was very short and intense and she let out a small cry of pain as her aching muscles tensed then released their grip.

She sat in the awning with a loose robe around her, not tied, but open, feeling the cool air on her skin, still tingling from the hot shower, a glass of red in hand, smoking her cigar, classical cd on, she was beginning to like this bohemian life. She looked down at her wayward pubes, they seemed to have grown even more: if she was about to go on a beach in her swimwear, they needed a serious cut and trim. Karen always used to make fun of her hirsuteness and said it was like sharing a flat with a monkey. Sally never took offence as Karen was the only person in the world, other than Dave, that she had been naked in front of, well at least in the daylight. Sharing a flat with someone for two years was almost like being married and although unlike Karen who would just wander around totally undressed there were never any closed doors in bedrooms and bathrooms, unless of course, Karen had a visitor! She put on her headset and turned the music up, took a large sip of wine and another puff of her cigar, she was feeling very relaxed and almost in a trance like state and closed her eyes for a minute: the exercise, the shower, the warming nutty flavoured smoke and the alcohol had started to take effect. Something caused her to open her eyes, she was aware of a noise and suddenly without warning, the flap of the tent opened and there stood Bryan and Janet.

"It's difficult to knock on these things, we did try to attract your attention from outside, but you didn't hear us."

She could tell they were surprised by the scene that greeted them, lying there basically naked, with a glass in one hand, cigar in the other, headphones on it was difficult to know what to do next. There was an embarrassed silence as she stood up to face them, she decided to play it as nonchantly as she could, not rushing to cover up or look upset. For their part they just stood there, not looking away as though what had happened was the most natural thing in the world.

"Sorry for barging in we just wondered whether you wanted to join us for dinner at the local pub?"

Sally was annoyed that her peace and solitude had been disturbed, was this typical of caravan sites, no privacy at all?

"No thanks, I'm eating in tonight, perhaps tomorrow?"

There was clearly no ambiguity about her response, she wasn't sure they understood, they had invaded her privacy and the annoyance in her voice should have left no margin for misunderstanding.

"Perhaps, see you tomorrow then?"

Sally nodded and they left. She wasn't sure if she had done the right thing in agreeing to meet them in Spain, but she could always change her mind. She poured herself another generous glass, wrapped the robe tightly around her and smoked her cigar in silence. She decided that the next morning she would pack her things and leave for home.

She was up early the next morning, somehow took down the awning and packed her things away; by 9.30 she was ready to go. She thought that at least she should say goodbye in person, however, the decision was taken from her as Janet suddenly appeared from the opposite direction from her van.

"Morning Sally, you aren't going, are you?"

Sally thought this was a rather silly question given the obvious circumstances.

"Yes, I have had a call from my mother, my father isn't very well and I am off to Bristol. I was just about to pop round and say goodbye."

She wondered if her lie had gone unnoticed, she didn't like upsetting people and they had only been friendly anyway.

"I've just been for my daily constitution, have you got time for a coffee; Bryan will have the first brew on already."

Sally wondered what her 'daily constitution' was: was it a walk or did she ablute in the site facilities rather than their own van. Perhaps Bryan didn't let her crap in the lovely van, Sally smiled at her own silliness.

"Yes, that would be nice, I don't have to be there until the hospital visiting time."

She was amazed how easily she lied, she had now become an accomplished liar to add to her list of slut, sexual deviant and God knows what else.

Bryan of course had got the coffee on she could smell it from ten yards away. He greeted her as though he hadn't seen her for weeks and kissed her on both cheeks, there was a warmth in the greeting that surprised her, she thought it was perhaps in the form of an apology for the previous day's invasion.

"Janet says you have to go to Bristol to see your father, is it serious?"

"Not really, although he has another mild heart attack and that's his second one."

Sally wanted to end the discussion about her father, one thing was for certain she needed to remember her lies for future reference.

"Are you still coming to Spain to see us, we don't want you to think we're interfering old farts."

She was a little surprised by the use of the word 'fart', the word 'fart' in her household when she was growing up was akin to a four letter word according to her father and she had never been able to use it as a result.

"No, I'm really looking forward to getting back to nature, the site sounds idyllic."

"I'll book it then and email you with the details, it will be absolutely great to show you the ropes for a few days, better bring your suntan lotion it's always good weather when we go and you don't want to burn your bits and pieces."

Sally thought it was an odd thing to say and couldn't think of a suitable response, she thought it might be as a result of the day before when they had seen her 'bits and pieces', so just nodded. She had a coffee and said her goodbyes, an hour and half later she let herself in her front door with a sigh of relief.

CHAPTER 6

THE BEAST

Over the intervening couple of weeks before her adventure, she taught herself to put up the awning, not in the military fashion of Bryan and Janet, but in a sort of 'one-handed' paper hanging sort of way. They were clearly not meant to be put up by one person, but after about three abortive attempts she found methods and ways to defeat the devil. At the fourth attempt she timed herself and was pleased to find that she could erect it in less than twenty minutes. She set herself a punishing regime of no alcohol, no smoking and at least a two hour bike ride or jog each day, cut down her calorie intake and was amazed that within a little over two weeks her weight had gone down by nearly a stone and her body had somehow gone back to it's old taut, muscular shape.

The Saturday before she was due to travel she had booked an appointment at her local hairdressers that also had a beauty salon attached and had decided that if a chap could have his 'back, crack and sack', waxed she could at least have her 'crack' sorted. At the age of 40 perhaps she should take more care of her appearance: she had discussed it with the beauty therapist, as apart from anything else, she was embarrassed, but the girl, who was only in her twenties, soon put her mind at rest and told her that she had 'seen it all before'. She asked Sally to take off her tights and knickers and put on a robe, she then asked her to lie on her front with her legs slightly apart. Sally could feel her lift the robe exposing her bottom. She was very pleased that she was lying face down as she was sure she was bright red. She felt the hot wax being applied and then almost at once it was ripped off taking the hair follicles with it. Sally let out a large cry, it was one of the most intense pains she had ever experienced, how anybody could be into 'S and M' she would never know. After about ten minutes she had to turn over and have the tops of her legs done, by this point she was far too much in pain to be concerned about embarrassment, she was really pleased that she wasn't going for a Brazilian, she was sure she wouldn't have coped with having the hair actually pulled from her delicate lips.

Arriving home, she made straight for the shower and felt the soothing luke-warm water cooling her, she sprayed it for a good five minutes over her very red bottom. She then shaved her underarms, something she hadn't done since she first went to university and felt the new smoothness. After drying herself she sat down with her back against her bed, legs apart and looked at her still very hairy crutch in the full-length mirror. The tops of her legs were still very pink but at least there wouldn't be any loose hairs escaping outside her bikini bottoms from that particular source. For one mad moment she considered shaving herself completely smooth and instantly her mind went back to a month or so earlier and could picture Maria's baldness. The thought excited her and she could instantly feel her response to the mental picture she had conjured up. She took a comb and a pair of scissors from her dressing table and started to comb her very long pubes, as she did, she trimmed over an inch from each pull of the comb until there was quite a collection of hair on her carpet. She very carefully cut around her lips and for the first time since she had been an adolescent she could see the very clear outline of her outer lips and liked what she saw. Her final act was to shave a very straight line from the ragged top of her bikini line. When she had finished, she opened her legs wide and admired her handy work, it was, she thought, like looking at an equilateral triangle or was it an isosceles? Her geometry lessons had always been a bit of a mystery.

She had booked an early ferry from Portsmouth to Le Havre on the Monday morning which meant leaving home about 6am and although it was a longer crossing than Dover to Calais, the overall mileage to Zurich was far less and Sally had decided to break her journey in Fontainebleau just on the south side of Paris. Dave and Sally had stayed in a converted Chateau there just after they were married and although the memory would no doubt be painful, she would enjoy reliving the past. Over the last few weeks she had begun once again to think more about him and how things could have been so different, if she had only just learnt to let go, somehow now, her new circumstances allowed her the freedoms she couldn't have even dreamt of before and it made her feel guilty – guilty, in as much as she couldn't enjoy it with the love of her life.

There was no doubt that she was excited and travelling along the M27 towards Portsmouth, this, as she had said to herself many times before, was the beginning of an adventure. The ferry ride to Le Havre went so quickly, that no sooner had she had breakfast it was time to dock. She drove off the ferry and turned on her satnav, she was lucky that the previous owners had invested in an all 'singing and dancing' European version. It showed both the old and the new numbers and driving out of Le Havre it told her to take the A13 and E5, she followed it all the way to Paris and having put in the details of her hotel, somehow, to her total astonishment it took her around the Route Periphorique and five hours later deposited her at the Chateau. She booked in and went to her bedroom: she was hoping that the familiar surroundings would remind her of happier times, but it was not to be and after a mediocre meal in the restaurant she retired early and was in bed at 9pm: after such an early start sleep came very quickly. She had set her alarm for 8.00 am as she wanted an early start and being a Monday morning expected reasonably heavy traffic. After the standard continental breakfast Sally gave Izzie a call.

"Morning Izzie, I'm just about to leave my hotel, I should be with you about 4p.m., I'll give you a call when I'm about an hour away."
    "Great, I can't tell you how much I'm looking forward to seeing you, drive carefully."

There was only about 300 miles to drive but Sally decided that she would take her time, have a bit of lunch on the way and enjoy the drive. This was the farthest she'd ever driven in her van and was really beginning to enjoy the experience of sitting a good two feet higher than most other motorists and couldn't believe some of the things she saw going on! Apart from the curse of the peage she basically kept going until about 3pm, when still 50 miles from Zurich she stopped for a snack and phoned her friend.

"Izzie, I'm about 50 miles away, depending on the traffic I should be with you in about an hour or so."
    "O.K. give me a call when you get to the apartment block, I need to open the gates and let your beast in. For God's sake hurry, I've had the gin and tonic on hold for the last two hours."

Sally couldn't believe how easy it was to follow the instructions coming from behind the dashboard, it even seemed to know its way around the fiendish Zurich one-way system. At precisely 4.30 she arrived at the apartment block. Izzie was there to meet her and opened the security gates. Sally parked the 'beast', (from now on that was going to be how she addressed her van), jumped down and embraced her friend. They were both totally overcome with emotion and they just stood there holding each other, tears streaming down their cheeks.
    "This is ridiculous, why are we crying?"

"I don't know, perhaps I'm missing the boys, although God knows why, they were a bloody nightmare all summer. I haven't quite got used to living here and every other week I need to visit my dad and Paul's always travelling. He's in Berlin all bloody week, every bloody week and only comes home on a Friday."

Sally had never heard her friend swear so much and was surprised how down she seemed.

"Never mind, I'm here now and we're going to have a good time."

"Paul's not home until Friday evening but he's organised for us all to go out to this brilliant restaurant and………."

"Come on, I could murder a G and T."

They took the lift to the third floor and Sally was amazed how large and palatial the apartment was, it was at least half as big again as Sally's cottage, she wondered how much Paul was earning. It was as though Izzie knew what she was thinking.

"Paul is getting on so well, it just pisses me off that he now works in Berlin all week, he might as well be commuting from the U.K. I don't have any real friends here although I've joined a sports club: you have brought your tennis kit haven't you?"

"Of course I have; the great thing about the 'beast' (she was getting used to Izzie's description), you can bring everything you want, it's like having your own house on wheels."

"Great! I've booked a court on Thursday from 4-6.; it will be like old times."

They drank and ate and talked and drank again. At 3a.m. Sally tried to stand up, eventually propping herself against the sofa.

"Izzie, I need to go to bed, I'm fucked!"

She was surprised at her own language, but that was the best and most appropriate verb she could think of on the spur of the moment.

They didn't get up until 11.

"I thought we could go into the city and have a late lunch. There are some great shops and we could either go out for dinner or eat in, what do you think?"

"I don't care, I'm just happy to be here." They drank about three coffees and then got a cab to downtown Zurich. They headed for Izzies favourite restaurant and spent the next three hours drinking and eating.

"My God Izzie I reckon I've put on a few pounds already it will be good to play tennis tomorrow."

They shopped for about an hour, Sally was not particularly interested and she had never been one for retail therapy, not a fashion guru, although always looking good: she was lucky that stuff off the peg used to fit her perfectly. After visiting the fifth shop she passed a Davidoff cigar store.

"Izzie, I need to go in and buy my father some cigars."

"Ok. I'll be in the boutique next door see you in a minute."

Sally loved cigar shops, no-one, she mused, who didn't smoke cigars understands what a wonderful smell the big walk-in humidors have. She walked in and was confronted by an elderly man, grey haired, well dressed; she thought he had probably been there man and boy.

"May I help you Madam?"

"Yes, I would like to buy a box of cigars for my father's birthday."

"Do you know what he likes?"

Sally knew exactly but thought she'd test him.

"I think he likes medium to strong, but I don't really know."

"Then Madam, if you would follow me into the humidor, I will explain the relative merits of the brands."

He spent the next ten minutes telling her about various brands.

"I would like two boxes of Davidoff Winston Churchills please."

"Two?"

"Yes I would like a box for myself. Can you arrange to ship one box to my father, is it possible that they will arrive by Saturday as I'd like him to have them for his birthday."

"Of course, Madam, anything is possible."

"Good, have you got some note paper, I would like to write a short message to him."

Dear Daddy

Please find enclosed a box of 25 Davidoffs, I know there not your usual Cuban brand but I like them, so being a daddy's girl, I thought you would. They won't make amends for all the ones I 'borrowed' as a rebellious teenager (I know you knew but as always, you were the sole of discretion), according to mummy and Doc Wallace you're only allowed one a week, so these should keep you going for six months, unless I come home at Xmas and help you! I'll keep mine in that beautiful 'jewellery' box you bought me for my 18th birthday. I know we shouldn't have secrets, but thanks for not telling mummy, I know she wouldn't approve, - so, probably not at Xmas then?

Having a brilliant time, please tell the silver surfer (mummy) that I will email my blog at the end of the week, I can't believe how she's taken to modern technology, she puts us both to shame!

Anyway, happy birthday for Saturday, really sorry I won't be there. Perhaps she'll let you have one!

Love and kisses
Your favourite daughter.
Sally xxxxxxxxxxxxxxx

"Where on earth have you been, I was about to send out the search parties."

"Sorry, believe it or not we got talking and the chap who served me, his son works in England, wanted to chat."

She lied again without thinking – why couldn't she just tell the truth she was beginning to get quite worried.

"How about we go and have a drink before we go back, or do you want to stay and eat?"

"To be honest Izzie a drink would be great but I feel really tired, can we eat in tonight?"

"I hoped you'd say that, I've got a load of stuff in the freezer, come on I'll take you to my favourite bar, we'll have a few drinks then go back to the apartment."

They spent the evening much as the previous evening, just talking, eating Pizza and downing rather too many red wines.

"You know Sally, I envy you sometimes, you are a free agent, you can go where you want, do what you want, think what you want."

For the first time since Dave's death, no-one had said that to her and although it might have been true, she'd never thought of it like that, she wasn't sure whether it was a good thing or not. She knew she felt the loss of Dave every day, she also hadn't had any children and at 40 something probably knew she never would. The remark from Izzie stung her somewhat, because, given the opportunity she would have swapped places with her anytime. She didn't answer, instead, stood up and went to the bathroom.

They got up again late on Thursday and had a late light lunch at the sports club before playing tennis. It was a very smart club and had a full health suite, swimming pool, restaurant etc.

"Paul and I spend at least one day a weekend here chilling, eating and believe it or not playing tennis. I have at last got him into it, he thought he was too old for squash, the trouble is I know it's only a matter of time before he starts to beat me and I don't know how I'm going to cope with that."

They played three full sets, Izzie just coming out on top, it was like old times, Sally was a bit rusty and it was obvious that playing with Paul had sharpened Izzie's game.

"Come on Sal how about a sauna, it's great fun, Paul and I usually have one, it's mixed by the way, but I know he likes looking at all the women, most of them are stunning and I don't care, unfortunately most of the blokes are old and fat with small cocks."

"Most men have small cocks compared to Pauls!"

Sally couldn't believe what she'd just said.

"That's settled then - let's go. I tell you what, let's play a game, we'll say Paul's is a 10 and every time a bloke comes in we will give it a score, for instance a really small one might be 3 or 4 while a large one could be 8 or 9. We'll just show a number of fingers to each other, it won't be obvious, we'll keep them in our lap and see how close we are."

Sally wasn't sure about sitting naked in front of everybody but considering her recent exploits was willing to give it a go and was feeling rather frivolous and the talk of Paul's cock had certainly livened her up.

They were sitting with two very old Germanic women, both with very large pendulous breasts and large tummies when the first man walked in. He was middle aged, good looking but with a very fat belly. Sally looked at Izzie and then both looked at each other's laps, Sally gave him a 5, Izzie gave him a 4. Sally thought the reason for that was that she hadn't seen Paul's prick recently and had forgotten how big it was. It clearly wasn't a good day for blokes, it was nearly ten minutes before two other young men walked in, both very well muscled. Izzie looked at Sally, the contrast couldn't have been more different. Izzie whispered to Sally.

"The one on the left, first."

They looked at each other's fingers, both scored a respectable 6. They then scored the one on the right, Sally looked at Izzie who opened her palms showing 10 digits but did it twice. They both looked down, not daring to look at each other, it was without doubt the biggest phallus Sally had ever seen and from Izzie's score, probably the biggest one she'd ever seen. After a few minutes they started to giggle and Sally could feel herself becoming slightly hysterical, she had to leave and take a shower. It was a unisex shower and as the girls stood there, 'bigboy' came and stood next to them, as he looked at them he used his hands to 'wash' himself all over, liberally handling his cock while looking at them, he knew what effect he was having. They both looked away and then mouthed at each other that they needed to leave and get dressed.

"Jesus! Can you imagine having that between your legs?"

"Probably, but I don't think it would be very comfortable, I thought Paul was well endowed but that was something else, I might start going to the club every Thursday if that's his night."

As they walked into the flat the phone was ringing.

"Hello darling how's it going?"

"You're joking, why can't you tell him to get lost, I can't believe you won't be home until Saturday morning, Sally and I were really looking forward to seeing you tomorrow, you know I'm flying off early Saturday morning, can't you change it?"

Sally was trying not to listen and went to the kitchen and made a couple of coffees, she could hear slightly raised voices, but gave them a good ten minutes before she heard Izzie put the phone down, she then thought it was safe to go back into the lounge.

"Sally I know you were going off on Saturday, but could you change your plans? You know I have to catch the 11am flight to London but Paul flies in at 10am, he's really upset he's not going to see you, what if you took me to the airport and then picked Paul up and spent Saturday with him. I really feel sorry for him, his boss is a real bastard and has insisted he entertains clients on Friday night."

Sally wasn't sure whether she should, she had been looking forward to being with them both on Friday, it would have been good to relive old times, wherever that took them.

But, what the Hell? She would really like to see Paul and she could always miss a stop-over on the way to Spain.

"O.K., I'll take you to the airport and pick Paul up, but I have to leave first thing Sunday morning."

"Brilliant, I promised to ring Paul back and let him know. Thanks Sally, he's working so hard I know he'd love to see you and I would be really grateful that he has a bit of company on Saturday. Regardless, we'll go to the restaurant we'd planned tomorrow, his fucking boss can pay!"

And that's what happened; they had a lovely day together and a fantastic meal in the best restaurant in Zurich. They spent the equivalent of £100 each in Swiss francs, they ate far too much and eventually arrived home at 1am, they then continued to drink and at 2am they went to bed. The room was spinning and continued to spin until Izzie woke her at 7.30am. As she drove her to the airport, she prayed that she wouldn't be stopped and breathalysed, she needed a coffee and even though she was less than 12 hours from eating, desperately wanted breakfast. They kissed and hugged and agreed not to leave it as long next time and would definitely get together before Christmas.

Sally went to the café and ordered a continental breakfast, croissants, ham, cheese, boiled eggs, black coffee. She looked at the arrivals board and noticed that the flight from Berlin was delayed by two hours and cursed. Just then her mobile rang.

"Hi Sal its Paul, I'm really sorry I won't get in until noon, sorry!"

"Don't worry, I've nothing else to do."

Sally was not happy, her head was throbbing and she felt rather hungover. She ordered another coffee and took some pain killers.

CHAPTER 7

THE SWISS AFFAIR

Driving him back, the atmosphere was a bit strained, it was almost like they were two strangers, they made polite conversation, at least she thought she felt rather better than she had, perhaps it was a good job that he was delayed. They continued to make small talk until Paul said.

"Right Sal what are we going to do, what about playing a bit of tennis and then we'll eat at the club restaurant, it's not five star but it's good and to be honest I've sat at my desk all bloody week and could do with a bit of exercise. Anyway, you should give me a good workout, Izzie said you nearly beat her the other day and I can't even get close to her."

The last thing Sally wanted at that moment was to play tennis, she wanted to lay down and sleep.

"Ok although I could do with a bit of a siesta, we only slept a couple of hours last night, what time were you thinking?"

"Not until later, I'll ring the club and see if we can book about 6, it's always very quiet on a Saturday evening."

Sally slept for a couple of hours until Paul woke her up with a gin and tonic at about 4 in the afternoon.

"Hair of the dog, don't want any excuses if I beat you."

They had a couple of drinks then took a cab to the club. She still felt that there was a distance between them and conversation was rather strained. As they went on court Sally couldn't help looking at the rather large bulge in his shorts. They knocked up for about 10 minutes before starting the game properly. He was powerful and Sally had difficulty getting back his serves, but after a few games that went with serve, got the measure of him and outplayed him with her strong forehand ground strokes. She won the first set 6-4. The second set was easier for her and she comfortably ran out the winner at 6-3.

"You're too good, shall we call it a day, I'm knackered, these business lunches and lack of exercise will kill me."

As they left the court they headed for their respective changing rooms.

"Heh Sal, how about a quick sauna before we eat, it would be nice to relax, what do you think?"

She did think! She thought she shouldn't. She thought….. God knows what she thought?

"Alright but I'm really hungry, just a quick one."

It was as though a 'quick one' wouldn't count, that's perhaps why they both referred to 'quick'.

They were the only two in there, they sat opposite each other. Sally looked down at her hands, her fingers and thumbs outstretched, it was as good as she remembered. She kept her head down, although her eyes, unseen, were looking at his long thick penis, as she stared at it she swore she could see it grow. Just then he stood up and with his back to her threw water on the coals. She felt the heat descend and could see the rivulets of sweat running down her body; she knew he was examining her. She was already excited, she could feel that familiar feeling, she wanted him then and there, she knew she was ready to accommodate him and knew she was as wet inside as outside. She wondered if he was feeling the same way towards her.

"Sal……?"

He was interrupted by a young couple which Sally thought were in their twenties coming into the room closely followed by two women, it was getting quite crowded.

Paul got up and indicated that Sally should follow him. They went outside and she followed him into the plunge pool, as they got in she could feel his body next to hers and it sent a shiver through her, although not as much a shiver as the icy cold water. After barely a minute they got out and walked to the shower. They stood facing each other, this time she made no pretence and looked at him, there was no question that icy cold water does have an effect but it was still big and thick and she wanted him more than ever, but knew with her friend away, she couldn't.

They took the lift to the third floor and Paul opened the door, as they went inside and before she could take off her coat, he tried to kiss her.

"I can't."

"Why not, you know you want to."

"It wouldn't be fair on Izzie, its one thing to include her, but this is wrong."

"She knows."

"What do you mean?"

"Nothing."

"What did you mean, Izzie knows."

"I shouldn't have said anything, forget it."

"You can't leave it like that."

He hesitated and there was an awkward silence.

"Ok but if I tell you, you have to promise never to mention it again."

She nodded.

"I might have suggested to Izzie that I wanted a threesome originally, but she was the one that pushed it and said she wanted to, as long as it was with you. She said she got really turned on at the thought of me fucking you and my God was she? You can't believe what she was like after the three of us got together. I obviously agreed as I have always fantasised about having you, I used to think about you all the time when we all went away together."

"I can't believe it."

"I bet she almost forced you to come back and stay with me today, she knows what will be happening now, tonight she will be wanking herself senseless at the thought of the two of us."

Sally was shocked but in retrospect it all started to make some sort of sense.

"But she told me that it was you and she only mentioned involving me, to shut you up."

"Look, I love Izzie and she knows that whatever I do with you won't make any difference to her and me, she knows we won't run off together, what a better arrangement could we have made? Don't be upset, we thought it might suit all parties."

"I really don't know what to say."

He kissed her again and this time she responded. She wanted him more than she had ever wanted anyone and had that familiar feeling again in the pit of her stomach that she had had in the sauna. He unzipped her dress and she let it fall to the floor, at the same time she tugged on his belt, she couldn't get his trousers and boxers down as his now stiff prick was sticking out at ninety degrees and causing an obstacle, they laughed at the ridiculous spectacle it must have been. He took off her bra, kissing and sucking on her pink, stiffening nipples and continued downwards, ripping off her knickers, then burying his head in her hairy muff, he was licking and kissing her and as he did, she stroked his head encouraging him to continue his exploration but instead he stood up, picked her up and took her to his bedroom, he threw her on the bed, parted her legs, there was no further foreplay, but if he was expecting her to be compliant he was in for a shock. She pulled him to her and told him to "fuck me, fuck me as hard as you can", she was shouting, she was foulmouthed.

"Fuck me with your giant fat cock you bastard! Get inside me, all the way, come on, harder, harder!"

He didn't hold back and gave her everything he could. After a few minutes Sally pushed him over on his back. She sat astride him, her black wet pubic curls mixing with his dark fuzz, she rode him as she used to ride her horse. She used her legs and feet as spurs, spurring him on to more effort, shouting as she rode him harder and harder.

There was never any question that they would climax together, they were as one. She shuddered as he shot his load into her, she continued to contract and release her muscles as if she was trying to milk the last drops from him. She was covered in sweat and could feel drips of water running down her side from her now very smooth armpits, there was a mixture of sweat, semen and her juice all mixed up in his and her pubes. They lay together on the bed exhausted, their coupling had been quick, but frenzied, the whole thing was probably over in less than fifteen minutes.

They lay in silence for half an hour, neither speaking. Paul was the first to shower. Sally lay quietly, not feeling guilty, although she knew she should. He came back to bed and she took her turn in the bathroom. She showered and douched with care, she hadn't taken precautions but hoped that at age 40 she wouldn't be fertile, it was too late now and that was the least of her problems. She returned to the bed and lay beside him.

"You know when we were in the sauna this afternoon I nearly had a hard on, thank God those two walked in when they did, trouble was every time I looked at you I just felt myself getting harder and harder, that's why I had to cool down in the splash pool."

"If you thought that was embarrassing, I was hugely relieved that I was sweating from every pore, it would have been rather bad if you'd seen liquid running down my inner thighs otherwise."

"I know this is personal, but have you shaved your fanny hair a bit?"

"Yes, don't you like it?"

"Like it, I absolutely love it! Izzie said you were always a bit hairy, I didn't mind one bit, it just seemed a shame that last time when I went down on you I had a bit of a job to find what I wanted."

They both laughed out loud. She looked at him, this time without inhibition or the need to hide her stare and slowly went down on his slightly stiffening cock and gradually brought it back to life, she kissed his balls and ran her tongue up and down his shaft, she suckled his spongy purple head until he started to get aroused. He immediately changed position and put himself in the sixty-nine position which gave him full access to her womanhood. His tongue found every orifice and as he licked and sucked Sally could feel herself about to come, no-one had ever done to her what he was doing. It was the most pleasurable feeling she had ever had, every nerve ending was alive to his careful and sensitive touch. He sensed her impending climax and stopped what he was doing; instead he pulled her towards him and whispered in her ear. It was as though he didn't want anyone else to hear.

"I want to take you from behind. I won't hurt you."

"Why should you hurt me?"

He knew from her remark that she hadn't fully understood.

"I want to fuck your gorgeous bottom."

This took her completely by surprise and Paul sensed it immediately but had already gone too far to turn back.

"Its ok, you don't have to if you don't want to."

"Its not that I don't want to, believe it or not, I've never done it."

Paul wasn't particularly surprised as he had only done it with Izzie a couple of times as she didn't like it. Somehow, he could never have imagined Dave enjoying it. Dave had always struck him as a straight sort of chap.

"I don't know; we are getting into territory I've never been to."

Although she hadn't with Dave, she had wanted to experiment but would never have dared to ask. Paul took her slight hesitation and lack of a totally negative response as a positive affirmation and reached over to his bedside cabinet and took a small tube of 'pina colada' flavoured lube.

"Sorry, but this is all I have, Izzie liked the taste."

She took it from him and squirted a large amount on to the palm of her hand. She rubbed her hands together and took his shaft and covered the entire length, finishing with the head. She then put some on the tips of her fingers and rubbed it liberally into her, knelt on the edge of the bed with her bottom exposed, knees slightly apart and head on the quilt and presented herself to him. She was slightly worried that she wouldn't be able to take him, she had tried a few times with 'Paul' but had never succeeded more than a couple of centimetres, but then again, she mused, she hadn't had a pina colada. He stood up and faced her offering; he opened her cheeks and felt for her opening, the light was poor, but he felt for the soft brown wrinkled skin and introduced his lubricated tip. She groaned as he tried to force his way in and she told him to be patient and slow down. She moved from side to side in an effort to accommodate him, with perseverance he slowly breached what had seemed an impenetrable entrance and with as little force as possible introduced his circumcised head. She squirmed and continued to move from side to side and very slowly and not without some discomfort for both of them, he began to force himself inside, after a few excruciating minutes when he was a few inches inside her, she asked him to stop.

"That's far enough; I can't take any more of you at the moment."

For a minute he didn't move, letting her internal muscles relax, then, when he felt the time was right, he cautiously started to move in and out, being careful not to force himself upon her. He was aware that she wasn't moving with him but 'stood her ground', he was more gentle than usual and, as he continued to fuck her, his hands felt for her breasts and very tenderly he held them, it was as if he was trying to counter one act of force by one of extreme tenderness; the sentiment wasn't missed by Sally and she responded by rocking backwards and forwards and from side to side, forcing herself to relax, she wanted all of him now, what she had, wasn't enough. He understood her mood and with ever increasing pressure forced his way in, she was moaning like a wounded animal, she slumped down on the quilt and opened her legs as far as she could, he placed his hands either side of her and took his weight and with extreme care he pressed harder and as he did she began to meet him halfway and thrust her bottom into him, inviting him to take all that was on offer and he did, finally accommodating about half but not all of his cock deep inside her.

They lay quietly like that for what seemed an age, as if neither dared to move. He eventually began to kiss her neck and back and as he did Sally started to squeeze her muscles, feeling for him again. He could feel the rhythmic contractions and he knew he was about to come but he didn't want to, using all of his will power he started to move his whole body up and down on hers, pushing into her again and then withdrawing. She groaned, but he knew this time it wasn't in pain, he also knew that he couldn't hold off too much longer. She came first though and when her climax began it started deep down in her belly, spreading like a wild fire, her fanny lips and clitoris quivered, sending shockwaves through her vagina, before racing onwards and inwards finally ending up in her bottom, rippling through muscles she didn't even realise she had, the waves came on and on like a rolling tide, her breath coming in great gulps of air followed by much shallower ones; she thought it would never end, she didn't want it to, but eventually she felt her body unwind and she stopped moving and was aware that he was no longer inside her, she couldn't remember him withdrawing but was glad that he had. She lay next to him, they were both covered in sweat, their breath still laboured, their hearts pounding. He turned her on her side, put his arm around her and drew her close to him; he kissed her passionately, like no-one had ever kissed her before, not even Dave. He pulled up the quilt and held her close: she knew in that moment the feelings she had for him weren't entirely sexual and she knew they were reciprocated.

They slept together all night, occasionally on waking she felt his breath on her, she would touch him lightly, lightly enough not to wake him. She didn't hear him get up and when she woke, he was standing beside the bed with a cup of tea in his hand.

"Thought you might like a cuppa."

He put it down on the bedside cabinet, reached down and kissed her on the lips.

"Did you sleep alright?"

"I woke a couple of times, but not for long. Will you tell Izzie what happened last night?"

"She already knows, I texted her from the club yesterday evening and told her that we'd played tennis and had a sauna, she's already texted me this morning and asked if we had a 'good time'."

"What did you tell her?"

"Enough, but not all."

"Sally, I………"

Sally put a finger to her lips.

"I need to get up, have a shower and get on the road if I am to get to Spain by Monday night."

He bent down and kissed her again but with more feeling, she didn't fully respond and he understood the slight rebuff. He knew, as she did, that there was no future in what had been left unspoken and the last thing Sally would have done is broken up the marriage of her best friends and anyway if this was a pattern for the future the last thing she wanted to do was ruin a perfectly acceptable arrangement. My God, she was even Godmother to the two boys. He kissed her again but this time on her forehead.

"You have a shower and I will get us some breakfast we can't have you driving a long way with nothing inside you."

The double entendre made them both smile; he left her to shower and went to the kitchen.

They kissed at the door as they said goodbye, he pulled her to him and she could feel him beginning to grow against her, she pushed him back into the room, unzipped him, knelt before him like a suppliant and took him once again in her mouth. She forced his manhood as far as it would go until it touched the back of her throat. She gagged a little before sucking on it long and hard, then withdrew, so she could look at the glorious monster, her lips enclosed around it once more and this time she sucked on the head using her lips and teeth to run up and over his rim. When he came, his juice spurted out in great globules covering her face and mouth, she swallowed hard and put it once more in her mouth, greedily gobbling, making sure she had every last drop of him.

CHAPTER 8

HAPPY CAMPERS

Driving out of Zurich she took the A1 through some of the best scenery in the world, passing by Lausanne and Geneva the motorways followed the lakes. Early on Sunday morning she had the road to herself, she also had her thoughts to herself and as she drove with her favourite music on reflected on the last year and a half and wondered what type of person she'd become. The first 100 miles flew by and she suddenly realised that she had remembered very little of the previous two hours, it was quite a shocking revelation and she chastised herself for not paying attention, unfortunately her head was filled with Paul, Izzie, Maria and Dave. Was she happy with what she had done? Was she happy with what she had become? Was she happy.......?

She picked up the main route to the South of France, the A7 at Lyon: had she been two months earlier it would have been mayhem, instead there was a steady stream of traffic heading south. Her destination was Montpelier, about 150 miles from Lyon a total of 350 from Zurich. She had originally planned to take an extra day but had absolutely no regrets about staying with Paul, the very thought of him gave her a feeling of contentment, she wondered exactly what Izzie knew and for a second she felt guilty, but then somehow, rationalised her feelings – Izzie started it! Mile after mile went by and in spite of only stopping for a few comfort breaks, to pick up fuel and those interminable peage stops she finally arrived at one of those national group of hotels that litter France. She had been driving solidly since 8.30am, it would have been 8.00am had it not been for a bit of unfinished business, but in the overall scheme of things she was rather pleased she'd stayed the extra half an hour! She parked up and walked into reception.

"Would Madam like to book a table for dinner?"

Madam would and thought that after a quick shower she would eat at 7.00pm, she realised that she hadn't eaten since breakfast, but what a big sausage that was! She actually laughed at the thought and realised that the receptionist, a po faced woman, who Sally considered to be in her late fifties, was staring at her.

"Sorry, 7.00 is fine."

She took the lift to the third floor and after fiddling with the plastic card opened the bedroom door. She threw her overnight bag on the floor, kicked off her shoes and lay on the bed. She couldn't get him out of her mind and instantly she pulled down her knickers and started to masturbate furiously; she opened her legs as wide as she could imagining him inside her, with both hands she probed and stroked both openings using her fingers; she was rough, ruthless even, and let out a small cry as she forced two then three fingers into her receptive cunt, within a couple of minutes she came, not as before, but quickly although nevertheless satisfying her basic needs. She lay quietly on the bed, the room was dark and almost at once she was asleep. The phone rang, she opened her eyes and for a moment had absolutely no idea where she was, slowly she took in her surroundings and after a number of rings, answered.

"Will Madam be dining with us tonight?"

She looked at her watch and saw that it was nearly 8pm.

"Yes......yes, I'll be down in ten minutes."

She couldn't be bothered to shower and went down to the restaurant: as she entered the restaurant and realised she hadn't properly eaten since that morning. Looking at the menu she decided on the 'plat du jour', three courses for 15 euros, a starter of soupe de poisson, a main course of coq au vin, followed by a plate of local cheeses. She wondered what it was about Britain that didn't allow restaurants to offer such great value. A large glass of the local red wine took the edge off her hunger and as she sipped not the smoothest wine she had ever drunk, she started to think how she was going to deal with Paul. There was no doubt that she had feelings for him that weren't only sexual and she knew that he thought the same about her, but there was no way she would 'rock the boat', but she also knew she wanted him again and soon.

She slept well, whether it was the drive or just a feeling of well being, she didn't wake until 9.00am. She only had less then 200 miles to drive before meeting with Bryan and Janet and really hadn't given a thought to her stay on the site in paradise, set amongst pine trees and sand dunes, - were they her words, or Bryan's description? One thing was for certain however, the weather, although warm was generally overcast and threatened rain, not the weather Bryan and Janet had promised at all. Before setting off she decided that she would call Izzie, whether it was a feeling of guilt or just to set her mind at rest she didn't know, but she was her best friend and still couldn't believe what had developed between her and Paul.

"Morning Izzie thought I'd give you a call see how your dad is," she lied.

"He's fine, in fact he's talking about coming out to stay with us for a while. Thanks for staying with Paul on Saturday he sounded like a different man when I spoke to him last night, I don't know what you did to him but it obviously worked, you'll have to come again."

Sally thought, if only she knew how many times, she probably wouldn't have said that.

"Have a great time with your new weird friends and let me know how you get on, I'm dying to know, I don't think they are quite what you think they are. Anyway, must go as I have a plane to catch in a couple of hours and dad's shouting. Bye."

Sally felt good that she had spoken to her, it was as though by speaking with her she had told her everything she needed to know and exorcised any possible guilty demons.

By 10 she had had breakfast and was ready to go, she had decided to take it really steady and have a long lunch, intending to arrive on the site by late afternoon. As she went from France to Spain there was a complete absence of any formal customs post, why was it she thought, that on the rare occasion she had arrived back in the U.K. there was always a huge queue for EC passengers, whilst potential illegal immigrants were given their own cubicle. Yet another conundrum that seemed to only effect the U.K. Driving into Spain she noticed a difference, they may only be a few miles apart but they were a world away in culture and custom, somehow, although her French was very good she felt that her spiritual home was Spain. Part of her degree necessitated a six-month secondment to Madrid University and looking back she realised that this was one of the happiest times of her life. She had fallen head over heels in love with her tutor even though she knew it would be unrequited, it was merely a silly fantasy. There was however something about the Mediterranean look, the dark hair, the olive skin and she often wondered whether there had been any foreign parts in her family, (although certainly no foreign parts near her mother)! Many times when she had been in Madrid she was mistaken for a native, she had always assumed it was her grasp of the language but she too had those dark swarthy looks. Sally decided to stop off in a small town and buy lunch, she parked 'the beast' in a picnic area and had a splendid feast, the van really was like having a home on wheels, she even had a lie down after lunch and instantly went to sleep, only waking up when some noisy Germans decided to park their monster van next to hers, in spite of having 'the whole of the rest of the f...ing car park'!

Eventually she found the site, her European satnav guiding her around various coast roads and villages, and to add insult to injury and for reasons she couldn't fathom the voice changed from a nicely spoken English Girl to a woman with a very strong German accent, she felt the 'beast' had been infected whilst she lay asleep in the car park. Never mind, the sun had come out and according to the temperature gauge in the van it was a rather respectable 24 degrees. As she drove onto the site, a large sign announced the name and underneath the name, 'Naturista' together with 'welcome' in about eight different languages, two of which Sally didn't recognise. She parked next to reception and walked in, there was a very pleasant woman behind the desk who spoke to her in very broken English. Sally responded in very fluent Spanish and instantly they formed a bond. Somehow, she knew who Sally was; she was of course the friends of Senor and Senora Higgins who apparently had been down to reception on the hour, every hour, since lunchtime. She gave her details, showed her passport, which was photocopied and signed in, there was, she thought, far more formality to this than entering the country a few hours previously, obviously international terrorists pick camp sites to plan their terror campaigns around the civilised world.

"Hello Sally."

Sally turned around and was confronted by Janet who was standing in the doorway without a stitch of clothing, totally stark naked, not even a fig leaf hid her parts!

"Hello."

Sally felt like screaming, she didn't know what to do, she looked at the receptionist who showed no emotion and suddenly she realised in that split second what a complete bloody fool she had been. 'Naturalist', of course not, he had said 'Naturist', had she not been pissed she would have known. What was the sign on the gate 'Naturista', it wasn't even that she didn't speak the language for God's sake. 'Don't want to burn your bits and pieces', my God, she deserved a PhD in naivety. What the f... was she going to do? Her mind was in total turmoil, she looked at the receptionist as if for inspiration.

"Your site is next to the Higgins, I'm sure the Senora will show you to it."

Regaining very little of her composure she looked again at Janet and said rather meekly.

"Christ, I could do with a drink, are you going to show me to my plot?"

Sally opened the door and let Janet into the passenger side, she knew the 'beast' had never seen anything like it, even with its slightly dubious previous owners.

"Had a good journey? Bryan and I were expecting you mid afternoon, never mind we're glad you're here now bet you can't wait to get out of those clothes?"

Sally couldn't bear to look at her naked passenger, instead just stared through the windscreen at naked cyclists, naked Frisbee players, naked barbequers, naked volleyballers (the last two verbs probably weren't proper words, but she didn't care), and even two couples playing tennis, just basically a whole campsite of naked campers! The site looked only slightly more than half full and Bryan and Janet seemed to have almost a whole corner to themselves, at least, apart from them, she wouldn't have many near neighbours.

"Park just there and I'll go and get Bryan, he'll be so pleased to see you."

Sally recoiled at the thought of a naked Bryan and was forming a plan of escape when no sooner had she parked he walked towards the van carrying a gin and tonic. She only hoped that it was shaken and not stirred. His willy was bobbing up and down on a rather bouncy scrotum, he hadn't a single hair on his body as far as she could make out but was the colour of mahogany. In that moment she likened him to one of those cheap bronze statues you could buy from pound shops for.... well, for a pound. She jumped down, he immediately handed the drink to Janet and embraced her, kissing her on both cheeks, she swore she could feel him on her leg, even through her skirt and inwardly shuddered.

"Janet, give the girl a drink she looks as though she needs one."

Never, thought Sally, had a truer word been uttered. Janet handed her the drink and for the first time since arriving she couldn't help but look at her 'new friends', they were beaming at her in what Sally considered, a slightly simple way. She was amazed however, how good the pair of them looked naked, in fact, especially naked! Janet had a trim figure although a bit of a tummy, but then again she had had four children she was entitled to, very neat breasts, thin hips and a very tidy trimmed bush, which was beginning to grey like her hair. Bryan was well muscled and obviously still went to a gym, slim hips and initially as she had noticed on arrival, a completely hairless body. She wondered why he bothered to either shave or wax, he was hardly an Olympic swimmer or cyclist. She tried not to look at his willy but couldn't help marking him using her and Izzies new scoring system, she wanted to give him a 4.5 but apparently half points weren't allowed, she would reserve judgement until she could have a proper look and knew there'd be plenty of time for that later!

"Come on Sally come over to us and sit down for a minute before we help you unpack and get that awning up, unless you want to change first."

By 'change' she knew he meant 'take your clothes off', no way was she ready for that, it was going to take more than a few drinks. Just as they sat down on their luxurious loungers a youngish couple walked past both wearing only a rolled up towel under their arm, bronzed and beautiful, she was going to look rather anaemic next to this lot, but that was the least of her problems!

"Shall we see you at the pool?"

"No, not today our friend has just arrived, and we are going to help her settle in."

'Damn', thought Sally she could have made good her escape, if not off the site then certainly somewhere, anywhere. She could feel a rising sense of panic, it was a feeling that felt like a lump in her throat, she took a very large gulp of her gin, nearly draining it in one go.

"Don't worry about me, you go and enjoy a swim."

"Oh, we don't do much swimming it's a real lively social scene, a lot of us come to this site the same time each year and every day at about 5 we head for the pool bar and have a good natter."

Sally conjured up the scene, it was something to be sitting in a mixed sauna naked, but around a bar with no clothes on with a load of strangers was clearly something else: she made a mental note to be out each day around 5. Perhaps they could sense her disquiet, Janet fetched her another drink which Sally was pleased to take, it was undoubtedly the strongest gin and tonic she'd ever had and wondered whether there was any tonic in it at all had it not been for a few lone bubbles rising to the surface. She was already getting a little light-headed and looking around her the whole thing was becoming a little surreal.

"Why don't you go and unpack and we'll be along in a minute to help you put up the awning"

What to do? She walked back to the 'beast' which was looking resplendent in the setting sun. Before making any decision she poured herself another drink in the rather vain hope that it might give her courage to strip off. There was, she decided, nothing else for it, she either got into her van and drove off or…… or, join in with the others.

"Have you got your awning out yet?"

She grabbed the canvas bag and laid it out on the sand in front of her van.

"I'll be out in a minute."

"No worries, we'll have this up in no time."

She went to her bedroom, took off her clothes and looked at herself in the mirrored wardrobe. She looked good and was glad for her recent weight loss, she couldn't stand their all day she had to make a move. Peeping through the window she saw the naked couple erecting her awning for her, as she peered at them Bryan bent over to pick up a stay and gave Sally a complete view of his bum and two dangly balls. She laughed so loud she knew he must have heard, which was confirmed when he turned around to look at where the noise was emanating from. She immediately ducked down and hoped he hadn't seen her looking. She knew her time was up and there was nothing else for it, although as she walked outside she grabbed her fold down picnic table she kept outside and carried it in front of her, it could of course only be a temporary measure, it would, she thought, look rather ridiculous if everytime she went out she carried a picnic table in front of her. There was however not going to be even a short-term reprieve, as no sooner did she get outside when Bryan walked up to her.

"Let me help you with that."

She had never felt so exposed, exposed in every sense of the word, not just her naked body, but she felt her very soul was on display for everyone to see! What did she do now? It was as though she had to do something different just because she had no clothes on. What would she have been doing had she got clothes on?

"Why don't we take you for a tour of the site?"

"Why not? I haven't got anything else to do."

Embarrassment wasn't a big enough word, they set off together in line abeam, passing other naked people and greeting them, it was obviously so natural to them all. First stop was the small shop; surely to God people weren't naked in there, were they? They jolly well were. Janet picked up a few provisions and joined the queue for the checkout, Sally counted eight people in line, an equal number of men as women, all shapes, all sizes, she saw that one's chap's member seemed to be poised over the woman's basket who was standing in front of him, it seemed to be peering in having a look at her shopping: Sally began to think she was hallucinating. Bryan and

Sally pushed past the queue leaving Janet to pay and as they did Sally felt herself touch another bare body.

"God, sorry."

"Don't worry, no harm done."

She thought if she didn't get outside soon she would start hyper ventilating, it was, she thought, one of the most disturbing events of her life. She took great gulps of fresh air as they got outside. Bryan sensed her discomfort.

"You haven't done this before have you?"

"No!"

"We thought not, look we're really sorry but we thought we made it clear what type of site it was when we met in Dorset."

"You did, it was my stupid naivety, I just can't believe I didn't realise."

"Why don't we cut short our tour, return to the van and have a cup of tea before we eat – by the way, the nights get a bit cool and we always dress for dinner, you will join us won't you?"

That was the best news Sally had received all day. Janet joined them and they didn't exactly march back, but Sally set a cracking pace and kept her head down.

"It's getting a bit chilly now the sun's disappearing why don't you put something on and join us in about an hour I bet you have loads to do?"

They watched as a bare Sally disappeared into her newly erected awning.

She couldn't decide what to wear and eventually settled for 'Dave's' pantaloons and a rugby shirt. Normally at home she wore nothing under them, but now she put on a pair of knickers, somehow it seemed appropriate after the afternoon she'd had. When she arrived, it was dark, but there was light emanating from the awning. Inside it was just as magnificent as she had remembered, the candelabra taking centre stage and beautifully decorated with cut glass wine glasses and gleaming cutlery. That wasn't at all a surprise, certainly not compared with Bryan and Janet! She was wearing only a longish tee shirt, although not quite long enough to cover her modesty and Bryan had basically a collared shirt, complete with tails, but it was obvious to Sally that both sets of genitalias would be on show the minute they sat down. They really had embraced the way of life!

"Gin and tonic?"

She remembered the last one she had and politely asked if she could have a wine instead.

Once again, as before, Bryan produced a meal that would not have been out of place in a five-star London restaurant. They ate and drank until finally Bryan offered Sally a coffee and liqueur, they got down from the table and relaxed in the fold up armchairs. She looked from his balls to her muff, clearly on display, however she didn't feel at all threatened and decided that she was obviously somehow getting used to all this nakedness but whether she could ever relax in a similar fashion was a debate she was yet to have. She thought they might be asexual, since she arrived there had been no innuendo, no deliberate double entendre, she felt very comfortable in their company.

"We're going off to a little beach tomorrow, it takes about 30 minutes on a bike, but it's really inaccessible and this time of year we might have it to ourselves, it's gorgeous, loads of sand dunes and pine trees, are you up for it?"

"I've nothing else planned."

"Great, we'll take a bit of a picnic, how about an 11am start?"

She said goodbye and thanked them for their hospitality. She arrived back feeling very mellow, she lay on her recliner, zipped up the awning and lit one of her Davidoffs, thought of her family, thought of her life, thought of Dave, thought of Paul and eventually went to bed a slightly disturbed but quite paradoxically, she mused, a very contented woman.

As forecast, the next day dawned bright and sunny and pleasantly warm. She looked out and was immediately confronted with naked bodies, just going about their business. It was too early to venture out without clothes and somehow she didn't feel quite as brave as she had done the night before. She suddenly wondered whether she was expected to cycle naked to the beach or whether it took in main roads or not. She decided that she wouldn't leave the van until it was time to go, she needn't have worried because at 10.55 they arrived, totally resplendent in their birthday suits and their mountain bikes, with bulging pannier bags. 'Shit' she thought, I'm not sure how cycling naked works, she could imagine 'swallowing' the saddle. Well at least she had her answer! She still had her clothes on, oh well 'in for a penny', she removed her clothes and stepped outside still holding a towel in front of her though.

"Let me take that for you, I see that you don't have any carrier bags, I'll put it with our stuff."

She instantly made a mental note that if this was going to be something she did on a regular basis she needed to get equipped; a lack of pockets was proving rather worrying. It's quite rough riding through the pine forest and dunes but well worth it when we get there."

They set off at a cracking pace soon leaving the campsite behind, she was in the middle looking at Bryan's bottom crack moving from side to side on his saddle and was rather glad that it was only Janet behind her. After twenty minutes she could feel the saddle rubbing against her bare bottom and far from any sexual feeling she was feeling a little uncomfortable and couldn't wait until they arrived. She began to think Bryan was a clairvoyant, it was as if he knew what she was thinking.

"Nearly there, just around the next corner."

It was so beautiful and as they had described the night before, a small cove set amongst sand dunes and, as predicted, totally empty. They left their bikes and found a suitable dune to deposit their bags. Bryan and Janet settled down to a bit of sun-bathing, Sally felt she could do with cooling down in the sea.

"I'm going for a long swim, try and work all the food and drink off I've been having recently."

She disappeared and headed down the beach towards the sea. She had forgotten how beautifully clear and blue the Mediterranean was and how warm it was for the time of year. She swam from one side of the cove to the other, a distance she thought was about half a mile, when she got there she was quite out of breath and decided that she would walk back. Her friends were hidden in the dunes but when she was about twenty yards away, she could hear them talking in low tones but couldn't hear what they were saying, she could also hear a smacking sound that she couldn't identify. When she was only a few yards away they came into view and what a surprise she had. Janet was laying face down in the sand, whilst Bryan was what could only be described as an intimate massage with a bit of smacking at the same time. She was moaning and telling him that she was a naughty girl, Sally ducked down and tried to make good her escape. Hearing her, Bryan turned around and stared at her, she could clearly see his excited state and there and then decided to give him a '6'. Janet immediately turned over and sat up, they were both now looking at her. She ran down the beach – 'so, they are asexual are they?' This was getting ludicrous, every situation she got into revolved around sex. She swam for ten minutes, long enough for them to sort themselves out. When she returned they were playing with a Frisbee.

"Good swim? We're probably going in a minute to cool down aren't we Janet."

It was as though she had caught them drinking a cup of tea, they seemed to have no embarrassment. She could see that Janet's bottom was quite red although there were no tell-tale signs of hand marks, he was probably good at it, it was not the sort of thing you wanted to parade around a nudist site. They were gone for about half an hour leaving

Sally to her thoughts. She didn't really have any, she was a little surprised by the turn of events, but it was hardly a criminal offence and was between two consenting adults, and, they were married, unlike her!

They had lunch and a glass or two of wine, they played Frisbee again, Sally wasn't sure about running around with no clothes on but it's amazing, she thought, how used you can get to something quite quickly. No more was made of the incident and after another swim they left at about 4, because as Bryan pointed out, it would be nice to introduce her to the 'pool' scene! She had already given up any thoughts of wandering off, this couple seemed to have a power over her and she was finding it harder to say 'no' to them. Perhaps for the first time since Dave died there was someone there to take control, it was unlike her not to maintain her independence. She was last in the line of cyclists and spent the next half an hour looking at Janet's red bum, she wondered what it was about 'S and M' that people liked, her only experience of pain was the recent waxing, which she certainly didn't find at all sexually exciting. Her fanny was beginning to ache with the constant rubbing on the saddle, she thought that when she got back she would need liberal amounts of moisturiser or just a long spray of cold water from her erotic shower. The thought of her genitalia made her think of Paul and within only a few moments she was aware that there was more than sweat on her saddle; she really wanted to get back but was beginning to rub herself up and down on her bike and fortunately, or unfortunately as they arrived on the site she knew she was about to come. She told them that she needed a shower, at, the very least some cool soothing water, naked cycling probably wasn't going to be her latest passion!

"So, you're Bryan and Janet's friend, we have heard a lot about you."

They had not so much as dumped her as sat her next to a chap they introduced as Vic and went off to talk to another couple. She went to shake hands with him, but he was having none of it and grabbing her shoulders, kissed her on both cheeks.

"Come and sit next to me and tell me all about yourself."

She really didn't want to but decided to give him a brief précis of her life so far. In response he smiled, showed remorse, laughed and barely said a word just letting her carry on. He kept supplying her with red wine and in the space of a little over a quarter of an hour she had downed two large glasses. Suddenly she stopped and realised that she was sitting next to a naked little fat man of about 60 with a small fat cock and had hardly noticed, he, on the other hand hadn't made her feel at all uncomfortable: there could be no question that nudity was something one got used to and she was actually beginning to find it quite liberating.

"You are coming to the 'Sixties Love-in' on Friday aren't you?"

"Sixties Love-in?"

"Bryan must have mentioned it?"

"Well, hope you come, you're obviously a liberal sort of girl, I'll go and fetch Sue my wife, she's dying to meet you."

Sally was getting quite worried and was wondering quite what Bryan and Janet had told them. Sue arrived a few moments later, a very large woman about the same height as her husband, but with massive breasts, large stomach, enormous bum, dark curly hair but one of the prettiest faces Sally had ever encountered.

"Hello Sally."

She gave Sally a massive smacker full on the lips, Sally felt her nakedness next to hers but wasn't at all repulsed, indeed it was a pleasant warm feeling.

"So, you're Sally."

Sally was beginning to think of herself as a prize cow. Sue must have realised by the look on Sally's face.

"Sorry, it's just that Bryan and Janet said that even though they had only known you for such a short time you seemed really nice, you know, one of us. So, what do you think of the site?"

"It's great, I've only been here for a couple of days but it's very relaxing."

"We started coming about ten years ago and have our own very secluded site behind the supermarket. It started with just a few couples but as we got to know more like minded people we agreed with the owners that we would have our own field. We come down every May and October and there are now about thirty couples who regularly come for the whole month. Trouble is we are all ageing hippies, children from the sixties; we could do with a few youngsters like you. Bryan and Janet normally join us but as you were coming down, thought they ought to go on the main site, anyway, have another drink."

The rest of the night degenerated into basically an old-fashioned booze up, she was introduced to more people than she could possibly remember. They were literally all shapes and sizes, she lost count of how many glasses of wine she had. The music was loud, the conversation was loud, the crickets were loud, in fact everything was loud, she could also smell cannabis, a smell she hadn't smelt for 20 years and the last thing she remembered was drinking a large glass of Spanish brandy and dragging on the largest spliff she had ever seen.

The sun was streaming through the open blinds: it was far too bright and what was that noise in her head? Where was she, slowly she came to her senses and in that moment she promised herself that she would never drink again. How on earth did she get home, she remembered nothing about the short walk home, she couldn't remember putting herself to bed. She made no attempt to get up or look at her watch, she felt absolutely wretched and wished for the time being that she was dead. She fell back into a restless sleep, waking occasionally feeling nauseas, this seemed to go on for ever and eventually her waking time became longer and her nauseous feelings less; she felt sufficiently strong enough to get up and have a drink of water. Looking at her watch she was amazed to see that it was 4 in the afternoon, she had lost nearly a day. She took a very long hot shower which seemed to revive her enough to face the outside world. Not bothering, she dried herself quickly and walked outside, loving the feeling of the sun on her naked body. Hunger was gnawing at her, she needed to eat, if it was at home she would have gone to the nearest McDonalds and treated herself to the biggest, juiciest burger she could find. Where was B and J, perhaps they felt as she did? Almost on queue they appeared, this was weird it was as if she only had to think of them and they turned up.

"Are you ok?"

"Yes thanks."

"We were worried about you, when we put you to bed we thought we ought to stay for a while, but Janet said you'd be alright."

Sally just looked at them waiting for more shocking revelations. 'My God' she thought, what did they do to me?

"Did I disgrace myself?"

"No more than anyone else, anyway everybody is looking forward to seeing you at the party."

Sally didn't find the conversation very re-assuring and thought it best not to continue.

"We're going into town on the bus, fancy coming?"

She didn't, she just fancied a quiet night in and something to eat.

"Sorry, but I don't feel up to it at the moment, I'll be alright tomorrow. Believe it or not I could do with an early night."

As it began to get dark Sally put on a pair of knickers and her old rugby shirt, made herself a huge fry up and drank copious amounts of water. Those OAP's just kept going; she couldn't even get close, best not to try. What though, had she let herself in for on Friday – she couldn't wait!

She decided that she needed a break from her new best friends and having taken a 'things to do brochure' from reception she planned to get up early on the Thursday and cycle to the nearest train station, a mere 10 kilometres and take a slow train into Barcelona. It was one of those old rolling stock carriages that stopped at every station and took one and half hours to travel only 30 miles, but she had time to kill and rolling through Spanish countryside appealed to her sense of adventure and it had been 20 years since she had visited that lovely city.

Arriving in the city at 11am it was time for a cortado, thick black espresso coffee with an equal amount of steamed milk, halfway between an macchiato and a cappuccino, she drank it and indulged herself with a sweet cake, not exactly a slimming breakfast but after her greasy fry-up the night before she yearned for something sweet and darkly satisfying. Gauldi was her first port of call, she hadn't seen it for such a long time and loved the avante-garde nature and quirkiness of the cathedral, she was neither amazed nor disappointed, it was basically as she remembered so many years before; she took in the sight and decided that she wouldn't go in, instead deciding that she wanted something simple, something to remember Dave, something to…. she didn't know what, but in that moment felt a closeness to him that had been absent for quite a time. Walking towards Las Ramblas she came across a small church, the doors were open and without hesitation she went in: it was cool and dark, the only light coming from a few lit candles, the eerie quietness and solitude and sheer spirituality of the place enveloped her in a comforting shroud, it was as if nothing or anyone could touch her. She wasn't religious but had a deep spirituality that had helped her through her sadness at losing the love of her life and without hesitation knelt in front of the altar and for a time felt a peace that she hadn't since that terrible day nearly two years before.

"Senora, do you need to talk?"

She looked up, and there standing in front of her was the priest, a young man with prematurely greying hair, although very attractive. Why were there so many good-looking priests? What a waste!

"You looked troubled would you like confession?"

Sally was troubled, troubled by the turn of events but being a lapsed Anglican and having never confessed to any of her sins she decided that this might be the time, in a foreign country and in a foreign tongue. She was uncertain as to what she should confess, she wasn't sure what she should say and she had only seen confessionals in films and on the television, but somehow it felt right.

"Yes."

She followed him to the confessional box, it looked just as she had imagined although it somehow reminded her of one of those passport booths. He asked her again what was troubling her, she hesitated not sure which sin she should own up to. She briefly told him of her life with Dave, his death and then.

"Forgive me Father I have sinned, (it sounded right), after I gave my job up I agreed to give lessons to one of my former pupils, Maria, she came to my house most Sundays and we formed a bond, unfortunately as the bond became stronger I began to have unnatural feelings for this girl..........................", she hesitated, she felt there was an air of expectancy from the other side of the curtain, she wasn't sure whether to continue or leave it at that, there was a silence before he spoke.

"If that is all then you did well to suppress your feelings."

"That's not all, I didn't suppress my feelings, when she passed her examinations she came to see me and I'm afraid I had sex with her, I wanted her more than I had ever wanted anyone, man or woman."

Sally pictured Maria standing there naked in front of her, her hairless body, her smooth fanny, her lovely bottom, her dark raven hair. Before he was able to say anything, she started again.

"I have to tell you more; I have slept with my best friend's husband while she was watching."

She didn't know why she had embarked on this course, it was surreal, bizarre even but perhaps it was a way she could put all of this behind her. But as she told him everything, she now saw Dave standing before her, but not with his cock, but with Paul's massive erect phallus in his hand willing her to suck and lick the purple helmet. She knew now she was a bit excited and without thinking her hand slipped down inside her skirt and started to touch herself, but suddenly realising where she was she felt totally ashamed, she knew instantly that what she had done was wrong, wrong on so many levels and rather than ease her pain she had now heaped her sins one on top of the other. He took a while to speak but when he did he spoke in short breaths, deliberately and slowly. Sally was in such a state she remembered very little of what he said or what she was supposed to do to absolve herself, she did remember promising never to sin in that way again. Walking outside in the warm, soft, autumnal air, was as invigorating as it had been minutes earlier when she had entered the cool, serene air inside the church. She needed a stiff one, in more ways than one – God knows what she had done, but in her mind she had reached some sort of watershed, a watershed of degredation. It was, she thought, quite the worst thing she had ever done.

She consulted her map and Las Ramblas was quite a way off, all she needed now was some retail therapy, forget this spiritual dimension, she was what she was and to Hell with it! She sat in a café drinking a large brandy and espresso, the open top bus route stop was across the road and she decided to spend the next few hours touring the city in total comfort, stopping and starting wherever took her fancy. She visited the normal sites and toured the city as most tourists do, having a tapas and yet another glass of rioja at every other stop. By mid afternoon she decided to head back and had made the decision to leave the camp site early next morning: the Friday night sixties love in was not for her and Bryan scared her, she had had enough of sexual encounters and the thought of Bryan smacking her bottom while Janet looked on filled her with horror. She still suspected that when they put her to bed the other night it wasn't as innocent as they made out.

She cycled back to the site just as it was getting dark, she was exhausted and all she needed was a nice cup of tea and an early night. The last few hectic days were catching up on her and the last thing she wanted was Bryan and Janet asking her out. Turning on the lights she slipped into 'the beast', took off her clothes and had a long warming shower. Looking at the erotica did nothing for her and after quickly drying herself she lay down on her double bed. There was shame, shame in what she had done in God's house, just shame!
"Hello, anyone there?"
She instantly recognised Janet's voice and her heart sank. Should she respond or make out she wasn't there. What was the point? No doubt they had seen her. Getting up she made no attempt to cover up and went to the awning and asked Janet in.
"Fancy a drink?"
"Thanks, a glass of wine would be good."
Sally noticed that Janet's voice was slightly slurred and guessed that the two of them had been at the bar. She had never before seen Janet in such a state of inebriation, the pair sat in Sally's awning, totally stark bollock naked and it seemed the most natural thing in the world. There was however something of an atmosphere, it was as though Janet wanted to say something but couldn't. They spent

the next hour drinking and exchanging small talk, Sally told her about her day and that Bryan and Janet had gone again to their favourite beach.

"Sally.......?"

"Yes"

"Bryan and I would like to get closer to you."

"What?"

"You know what I mean."

Sally did, absolutely and categorically, but didn't want to go there.

"Sorry Janet I'm at a loss."

This was getting more and more difficult; Bryan clearly hadn't got the balls to say it. Sally might have had more respect if he had turned up, but to send his drunk wife to proposition her was a tad too far. There was a terrible tense silence where no-one spoke. Sally could stand it no longer and decided to take the 'bull by the horns'.

"Janet, I suggest we have another drink and let's stop the bullshit."

She poured two very large glasses of wine and handed one to Janet.

"Janet, you and Bryan have been really nice to me, you have gone out of your way to be friendly but that is as far as it goes. I know what you are suggesting but I have no interest, I'm sorry, I don't know what to say."

Janet downed her glass in one, stood up and without any niceties said goodbye, leaving Sally still sitting in her lounger. Sally knew she had to pack, tomorrow she would leave, Friday sixties club would have to wait: she looked at her full glass of wine still on the table and somehow couldn't bring herself to drink it.

She planned her escape, it wouldn't take long to put the awning away, it was a lot easier to take it down than put it up and the beauty of having your house on wheels meant that you only had to turn a few things off and bolt a few things down, she reckoned she could be ready to go in less than half an hour. She had picked a beach site halfway between where she was and Alicante, only expecting to stay the one night as she had told Karen that she wouldn't be arriving until the Sunday and not wanting to change the arrangement was sure that she would have no trouble at this time of year arriving one day earlier than expected. There was now a clear awkwardness between her and Bryan and Janet, one which she didn't feel at all responsible for, but even though she knew she was being childish decided that she wouldn't say goodbye. She started to tidy 'the Beast' and give herself less to do in the morning, she would set her alarm for 6.30am and aimed to be away for 7.30am, hopefully before the site was properly awake. The rest of the evening she would spend catching up with Izzie and her Mother.

Waking a few minutes before her alarm, she got straight up, put on the kettle and within about fifteen minutes had managed to dismantle the awning and nearly get it in the bag provided – why on earth did they always make the bags slightly too small? By the time she had drank her tea it was beginning to get light and by just after 7 she was ready to leave. She had enjoyed her stay it was a great pity how it had ended on a slightly sour note.

CHAPTER 9

HERE COMES THE JUDGE

It was an easy drive, albeit entirely motorway and slightly boring but it took far less time than she had imagined and by mid afternoon she was on the site. As she drove in she was relieved to see that everyone had something on. She explained to the receptionist that she had arrived a day early but, as expected, it didn't present a problem and she was given a small site plan and a plot number. Sally had picked the site as it was quite close to the motorway yet backed onto the beach; it was only to be a short stop so she hadn't wanted to go off the beaten track. Her initial view of the site was pleasing, her plot was very nice and she didn't have any immediate neighbours.

Once she had the van in position she went for a walk along the very sandy beach. There were very few people on the beach, some families with small children, obviously taking advantage of the cheap out of season prices. It was hot, much hotter than it had been 250 miles further north and after ten minutes Sally could feel herself starting to sweat. As she walked farther along the beach away from the site she had the whole beach to herself, walking for another fifteen minutes she could barely see them in the distance. Immediately stripping off she waded into the warm clear water, it was such a good feeling after spending the last four or five hours in 'the beast'. She swam very hard for a good half an hour and was surprised how out of breath it made her; she certainly wasn't as fit as she had been when she was at school. As she got out of the water she noticed how ragged her pubes had become and made a mental note to sort them out before she got to Karens, it was bad enough that she used to call her 'monkey', she didn't want to give her any excuse to resurrect the nickname. She also noticed that both her breasts seemed slightly swollen and a bit tender, it was probably the sudden exercise and the fact that she had been exposing them to the sun for the last week, perhaps she should be a bit more liberal with the sun cream. Not having bought a towel she carried on walking, drying off in the late afternoon sun, eventually she came to a rocky headland and as she rounded the corner there were two teenage boys fishing from the rocks, right in front of her. She wasn't sure who was more surprised; she could only have been feet from them. They stared at her making no attempt to look away. Sally spoke to them and asked if they had caught any fish. They shook their head without saying a word. She said 'goodbye', turned around and walked back towards the site, she resisted the urge to turn around almost knowing that they would be looking at her, although here in Spain nudity was not such an unusual sight. Once she was far enough away and totally dry she put her clothes back on and made her way back to the camp site. She realised that she was extremely hungry only having had a small snack mid morning.

The heat inside 'the beast' was stifling, in her hurry to get out she hadn't opened the sky lights and having already made the decision not to attempt to put up the awning she took her chair and set it up outside, taking with her a very nice crisp cold white rioja she had bought from the shop on the previous site. She took her phone as she hadn't been able to ring her mother the previous night as she had been on the phone to Izzie for over an hour and by the time she finished her parents would probably have been in bed. Thank God, Izzie insisted on ringing her back saying that Paul's company paid all the phone bills and were used to international calls. It was so good to hear from her best friend and was certain, although nothing had been said directly, that Izzie knew what she and Paul had been up to but perhaps not in graphic detail. But if it did them all a good turn long may it continue. Izzie asked if Sally would still be travelling in November and if she was it would be great if she could time it so she could be with them both on Paul's birthday on November 15th. Sally said she probably would but didn't commit herself saying that she'd ring later.

As she picked up the phone to ring her mother she noticed she had two unanswered text messages. The first was from Bryan and Janet, as was the second.

'Surprised you went without saying goodbye.' Time 8.10am.

'Don't know what to say we obviously misunderstood the signs, sorry if we offended you, please text back.' Time 4.13pm - only half an hour ago.

What signs had she given off? None that she was aware of. She had done her best not to encourage any sexual innuendo or impropriety – hadn't she? Should she text or not? Oh to hell with it life was too short and she didn't have to see them again.

'Thought it was time to move on, didn't want to be in one place too long, hope you have an enjoyable rest of your holiday.'

Hopefully that would be that.

She rang her mother as she had done every few days since she had been away and, as always, very little to report. Father's stents in his heart seemed to be working well and he was back playing 18 holes and 'living down the bloody golf club and when are you coming home, I miss you.' Being an only child was quite a burden and it made Sally feel guilty, they weren't getting any younger but while they were relatively well she wasn't going to indulge them too much.

Her evening meal consisted of a fridge clearance, she wanted to make sure all perishables had gone when she arrived at Karens. It was one of the best meals Sally had ever eaten, whether it was as a result of her gnawing hunger, or the fact of the relief of escaping from Bryan and Janet she didn't know but the combination of meat, fish, vegetables, cheese, fruit and a few miscellaneous items was a veritable feast, she only left some bacon and a few eggs that she would consume the next day. She emptied the last of the rioja and suddenly realised she had drank a whole bottle in less than two hours, she knew she really ought to cut down but at that moment nothing could have been further from her thoughts, taking the glass she went again outside, it was quite dark and apart from a few children still playing the site was still. It was warm and the night air gently caressed her slightly sunburnt skin, she felt very content with the world.

The next day passed pretty much as the previous afternoon, she took a long walk, swam and dried in the sun, by mid afternoon she walked into the village a couple of miles from the site. It was she thought like walking into a Wild West town only the brushwood was missing. There was one small bar which was also the village shop, it was much fuller than she would have thought, mainly with older men, then she realised that it was Saturday; they had probably sent their wives into the next town while they enjoyed a drink. There was obviously no table service, so she ordered a coffee at the bar and took it a table outside, there were ominous rumblings from the distance, and she noticed some very dark thunder clouds that seemed to be heading her way. She had intended eating out, having consumed the contents of the fridge the day before but there was no where to eat unless she went into town and she really couldn't be bothered to unhook the van and drive. She bought some bread, cheese, chorizo and ham and decided to have a simple meal in. The wind was beginning to pick up, a sure sign of an approaching storm and the sky was becoming darker by the minute, she reckoned it was half an hour walk back and decided to chance it. About ten minutes into the walk the rain drops started to land, large drops that splashed in the dust on the dirt track road kicking up spurts of filthy water, within a few minutes the thunder and lightning seemed directly overhead, by now the rain was torrential, there was nowhere to shelter it was just a dirt track road that was quickly turning into a river of mud. An old truck rumbled past throwing a huge amount of muddy water over Sally, she was now very cold and very fed up, she reckoned she still had about a mile to go when a car pulled up alongside.

"Jump in."

It may have been a mass murderer for all she knew, but she cared not. In the driver's seat was a young man, she put him at no more than 30, in the back were two pre-school kids, probably 2 and 3.

"Saw you arrive on the site yesterday and then saw you having a swim yesterday afternoon."

That was impossible, she had been totally alone.... as if reading her thoughts he said.

"We take the kids to the dunes, we all like to go back to nature once in a while."

Sally coloured up at the thought of being spied upon, at the thought of examining her pubic hair, her breasts and God knows what else she did.

"Oh," was all she could think of saying.

They were soon on the site and as he dropped her off she thanked him profusely.

"Thanks, that was really good of you."

"No worries, I'm your next-door neighbour anyway."

With that he drove all of twenty yards and parked next to a very nice caravan.

She threw her soaking wet clothes on the floor and walked into the shower turning the heat up as much as she dared without scalding herself. She stood there for a good five minutes slowly warming her body and beginning to feel human again. Drying herself she noticed again her wayward pubes and decided to cut and shave them. She laid a towel on the end of the bed and sat facing the full length mirror, legs wide apart, first she combed and cut off more than the previous time, until there was a thick pile of black curly hairs on the towel, next she gently gelled around the top of her legs and then rubbed gel into the bottom half of her lips. Very carefully she shaved around her legs and then, with even more care, shaved around her lips, by the time she had finished she could clearly see her outer lips, pink and smooth - now let Karen call her 'monkey', although, she still had more pubic hair than most women and left a nice thick black triangle finishing halfway down her crack. She should of course have had a shower afterwards, not before, never mind she went back in and did totally disgraceful things with the shower head until she was totally clean, inside and out. She really did love 'the beast' and its equipment, it had almost taken on a persona and she often found herself talking to it.

The thunderstorm had long gone and the sun had made an appearance, sitting outside she felt human again, a glass of red in her hand and everything was ok. The rain had somehow cleared the air and although it wasn't as warm as it had been there was a lovely clean feel about the place.

"Hi, I'm Lee."

She looked up and there grinning at her was her saviour from a couple of hours before.

"Hi, look I meant to come over and thank you properly, I don't know what I would have done if you hadn't come along. Would you like a glass of wine?"

He looked anxious, as though by agreeing he would be committing a terrible betrayal. He looked at his watch.

"OK, just a quick one, Helen will be back in a minute she has just taken the kids swimming."

She poured him a beer as he preferred this to the wine on offer. There was a little awkwardness, though once he had downed the second glass he became more talkative.

He talked about his job, which he was unhappy about and told her about his evening class in sports and injury massage. His intention was to build up enough private clients to be able to give his job up as a legal executive. He told her that he already had ten regular clients but needed at least forty before he could make the break. Suddenly he stopped talking, looked at his watch and stood up.

"Look, I go for a swim every morning at 7am before the wife and kids get up, how about joining me tomorrow, I'll knock on your door."

"Um...."

"I have to go, I'll knock anyway."

He was gone in an instant like a scalded cat, not two minutes later Sally saw the kids appear, then the wife. That was the reason. She disappeared into her van to start her evening meal.

True to his word he knocked on her door at 7 the next morning, she was waiting, she gathered up her beach towel and followed him outside.

"I usually jog, it's only about half a mile, are you up for it?"

They were in the sand dunes within five minutes. He stripped to his trunks and ran to the water's edge, she followed him, prudently dressed in an all in one swimsuit. They swam hard for a good half an hour before returning to the dunes. In front of her he took off his trunks and dried himself.

"Would you mind turning your back, I'd like to take my wet things off as well."

He did but only momentarily and before she could hide her modesty he turned around and stared at her.

"Hey, I asked you to turn around."

"Sorry thought you'd have your towel around you by now."

He made no effort to look away. Sally was cross and turned her back on him.

"How about a massage, I'm always looking for people to practise on."

As much as she liked a massage she thought this was not a good thing to do at the moment.

"No, your wife and kids will be up and wonder where you are."

They jogged back in silence and as she stopped at her van he casually said.

"Same time tomorrow?"

Before she had time to answer he was gone.

She spent the day reading a novel, walking along the beach and cleaning the 'Beast', just generally relaxing. There was no question the early morning exertions had done her good and she felt fitter that she had done for a while. She would go with him tomorrow.

She lay on her towel in her wet swimsuit making no effort to get changed, there was a cloudless blue sky and although the sun was barely over the horizon it was warm.

"Don't worry about me you go back to your kids."

"I'd rather give you a massage."

He was, if nothing else, persistent.

"Go on, my tutor told me I have to practise, practise practise!"

"OK, but I'm keeping my swimming costume on."

She lay on her front on her towel. What followed was the most amazing massage she had ever experienced. He did pull her shoulder straps down but stopped there, when she turned over he covered her breasts with his towel and although his hands explored right up to, but not including 'out of bounds' he knew what he was doing. She knew if he had tried anything else she would have undoubtedly let him. His touch was light yet strong at the same time, he really had a gift and she did not want it to stop. Suddenly without warning he looked at his watch and with panic in his voice said that he needed to go. He left her lying in the sand all alone.

Later in the day as he was taking water back to his caravan he stopped and merely said.

"6.30 ok tomorrow?"

She nodded, she knew exactly why he suggested so early, but was rather looking forward to another massage.

She lay face down again but this time made no protestation when he removed her costume. Whatever signals she had given off the day before he had picked up on them, his hands were firm, yet gentle, he massaged her back, her legs, her bottom and then turned her over. She was surprised that he too was naked but in spite of the situation his cock was limp. She closed her eyes and let him work on every square inch, his hands stroked and squeezed her breasts, teased her nipples then slowly began to work on her thighs and genitalia. She kept her eyes closed, she was in a dream like state, she didn't want him to finish, his fingers explored her but this was not like a sexual encounter it was something altogether different. He ended by covering her with his towel and gently kissing her on the forehead.

"I hope this isn't the usual massage you give, what sort of sports injury would I have had?"

She noticed his cock was still limp and somehow she never felt threatened by him.

"Hope you enjoyed it, got to go, same time tomorrow?"

And so it continued, each day it got better and better, they would now swim together without the need for swimsuits and there was a growing intimacy, he did things to her body that made her feel totally oblivious to her surroundings. Somehow though she knew they would never have intercourse, not once did she see him erect, nor had she touched him. She climaxed many times each time she had a massage making no attempt to hide her feelings, he could almost make her climax at will.

"Tomorrow is your last day, I want to make it very special for you."

Sally was excited at the prospect, like a silly school-girl she could barely sleep, she knew he wouldn't try to fuck her, indeed his cock was constantly limp and lifeless, she was also glad that there wasn't the added complication of full blown sex. She couldn't understand how he could possibly make it any better, she couldn't believe he could make her come any more times than he had that morning. She was restless all night waiting for the knock on the door at 6.30. As a result she overslept and the loud bang on the door made her jump. She ran to the van door and opened it.

"You slut!"

"What?"

"You have been having sex with my husband, he's told me all about it, how you seduced him. Just because you haven't got a husband there's no need to steal mine!"

The woman was small, dumpy and very plain – Helen. The veins in her neck were standing out and she was red faced, for a moment Sally thought she was going to be attacked.

"Stay away from him you bloody tart!"

She slammed the door leaving Sally standing there shaking. The incident had only taken a few seconds in which time Sally hadn't said a word or had the chance to defend herself. One thing was for certain however, looking at her no wonder he never had a stiff cock!

She eventually arrived at Karen's apartment block, having religiously followed her satnav around the back streets and one-way system in Alicante. Karen was waiting outside and indicated to Sally where she should park her van. Seeing Karen again was like the intervening twenty or so years hadn't happened they just seemed to pick up where they had left off.

"I thought we would eat in tonight if that's ok? Didn't think you would want to go out after a long drive."

"No, that's fine anything you like."

The next few days passed in a complete blur. They ate out at lunchtime, if they got up in time, they ate out at dinnertime if they didn't and sometimes forgot to eat at all, they went to bed at two in the morning and one night, not at all. It was as though they were at University again, neither with a care in the world. Shopping trip one minute, tapas the next, the beach one afternoon, the sports club another, although Sally still wasn't sure why Karen had joined as the only sport she seemed keen on when they were at university may have involved balls, but certainly not the ones you hit! It was obviously a good social scene, although according to Karen she hadn't managed to 'pull' anything since Miguel had left.

"Sometimes Sally, a good wank just doesn't do it!"

Sally knew what she meant, although before Paul, a good wank seemed to be enough.

"Right Sal, Friday night we are going to my favourite restaurant so let's get up late have a bit of lunch, then eat late, is that ok for you? It was mine and Miguel's favourite place and just because we've split up doesn't mean I have to stop eating there."

When they arrived at the restaurant right in the middle of Alicante Karen was welcomed by the head waiter as if she was the best customer they had ever had.

"Great to see you again, it's been far too long, where have you been hiding?"

She made some excuse about travelling which seemed to satisfy his curiosity and he showed them to their table.

"The one you always have; how is the Senor?"

"Oh, he's well; he is away on business at the moment."

This actually wasn't a lie as he was in Cuba on one of his many jaunts and no doubt whoring his way through Havana!

They had, as usual been eating and talking without stopping for a couple of hours, they weren't really aware of anyone else around them. Sally glanced at her watch, it was 11pm but there were still people coming in to eat, she had forgotten how late the Spanish ate. They finished their coffee and Karen called for the bill.

"Where are we going now then Sally?"

Sally could have done with going to bed but wasn't going to be a party pooper. Before she could say anything the waiter re-appeared and spoke to Karen.

"The gentleman that was sitting over there has asked if you two senoras would join him for a coffee in the lounge."

Both girls had been aware of a very distinguished grey-haired man in his sixties sitting on his own in the corner, they had mentioned him when they arrived as he was the only other person in the restaurant at the time.

"What do you think Sally, we hadn't got anything else planned, won't do any harm to have a coffee, anyway, I'm intrigued."

They followed the waiter to the lounge, a splendid room with leather seats where patrons could indulge in a post prandial drink and smoke, it reminded Sally of her father's club in London. As they approached him he rose from his seat and greeted them with a perfunctory hand shake and a kiss on their cheek. He introduced himself simply as Luis and asked them to take a seat. Karen thought he looked vaguely familiar but as with a lot of well bred older Spanish men they seemed to have a typical look and style and she thought no more of it.

"I'm drinking this rather splendid 30 year-old brandy, could I interest you in a glass?"

Without waiting for a response he indicated to the barman.

"Now then Senoras, why don't you introduce yourself."

There was something rather mesmeric about him, he was clearly a man who was not only used to giving orders but expecting them to be carried out. He was quite small but had a lot of silvery grey hair, beautifully cut, Sally thought his suit and shirt would have cost thousands, he was quite simply, immaculate. The drinks arrived, probably the largest brandy balloon Sally had ever seen. They drank in silence for a moment before Luis spoke again, it wasn't as though he was interrogating them but they found themselves telling him far more than they intended and as the second Brandy went down both girls had basically told him their life story, whilst for his part he had told them very little.

"Can my chauffeur take you home, or would it be too presumptuous of me to ask you both back to my house for some more of this wonderful brandy, it's my particular favourite and I always carry a large stock. My house is only a few miles away and it seems such a shame to sit in this dark room when we could sit in my courtyard and take in the views on such a lovely evening."

They neither agreed nor disagreed.

"Good."

He stood up and indicated that they should follow him to a back door where a large black Mercedes was waiting. A uniformed chauffeur opened the back door for the girls and Luis sat in the front.

"We haven't paid our bill."

Without looking at them he merely said.

"It's taken care of."

Sally whispered to Karen.

"What are we thinking of, he might be the mad axeman for all we know."

"Come on Sally where's your spirit of adventure, I told you we were going to have a ball, let yourself go for once.

Sally thought if only Karen knew how far she had let herself go in the last twelve months she wouldn't have said that. They arrived at a very spacious villa a few minutes later, it was very well lit and there were two sets of gates that the car had to go through before it came to a halt in a very large courtyard. It was like a fortress Sally began to panic as she realised that without help there would be no way to get away. Karen sensing Sally's disquiet linked arms with her and walked through two enormous oak doors into a hallway lit with a magnificent chandelier hanging from the ceiling, 30 foot above them.

"My butler will show you into the drawing room and get you a drink, I have a call to make, I will be with you shortly. They followed him up a central staircase onto a huge galleried landing and were shown into a drawing room not unlike the room they had left at the restaurant. The butler slid back a door which opened onto another courtyard and before them was a view of the whole of the city they had just left with the sea twinkling in the light of a nearly full moon.

"My God, it's breathtaking, this guy must be serious wealthy!"

They sat down taking in the view.

"Senoras, can I interest you in a drink?"

"I don't think I better have another brandy, I would just like a soft drink please."

Karen nodded in agreement, a moment later the butler re-appeared with two glasses of wine and another brandy and was followed by Luis, either he had misunderstood or just chose to ignore them.

"That will be all, thank you Juan, if you just leave the bottles here I will deal with it now, goodnight."

"Goodnight Sir."

The three of them sat in silence, all they could hear was a faint hum of the traffic in the city and the odd dog barking.

"Beautiful, isn't it, I am a very fortunate man."

The conversation was becoming a bit stilted, both girls took a large sip of their wine, Sally was definitely feeling a bit drunk as they had basically been drinking on and off for most of the day, she was unsure that if she said anything it would come out right, especially in a different language.

"Shall we go inside it's getting a bit chilly out here." There was never any real question whether they would go in or not. Luis rose and walked into the room, as he did, he picked up the red wine and emptied the bottle into their now empty glasses. He put on some soulful jazz and sat down in the big leather armchair.

"Senoras' I have always found that it is best to be direct. I am a man in my early seventies and certainly not getting any younger, I love the company of beautiful young women they make me feel young again. I would very much like it if I could make love to both of you."

Karen started to say something but was cut short.

"I am also a very generous man and I wouldn't expect either of you to give up your evening for no reward. I will leave you for a minute to think about it. Please don't be offended and my chauffeur is available if you chose not to take my offer……by the way there is a cloakroom down the corridor."

Sally just looked at Karen in a state of shock.

"Ok, what do we do now."

"Well I'm up for it, I don't care how old he is, he's very charming and I haven't had a shag for over a year and you haven't either, what are we waiting for. Come on Sally you can't be that naïve that you didn't know why he asked us back."

Sally didn't know what to think, she was almost too drunk and tired to bother, she did know that this was becoming a complete re-run at her time at University with Karen.

Karen got up to leave the room.

"Where are you going?"

I'm going to have a shower, where are you going?"

To call it a cloakroom was a complete understatement, it had a very large walk-in shower, a claw foot enamel bath, a bidet, two sinks and a toilet in a separate room. Karen stripped off and turned on the shower.

"What are you waiting for?"

Sally was beginning to think that she was in a totally untenable position and was regretting meeting up with

Karen. There was nothing else for it, she either had to join in or ....what?

Both girls dried without saying a word, they put on their high heels and looked at each other.

"Come on monkey, you look stunning with that all over tan, let's give him what for".

Sally knew to what Karen was referring to and even though she had spent money and time on her intimate grooming, she still had a big black mass of curly pubic hair, in spite of her ministrations the previous week. They walked towards the drawing room and when they entered the room the lights had been turned right down and Luis was sitting on the sofa wearing an open neck shirt, a pair of casual trousers, and a pair of very expensive looking shoes.

"My goodness you are both absolutely beautiful why don't you join me on the sofa?"

They sat either side of him, he looked at both in turn and then without saying anything placed his hands on their fanny's although he made no attempt to explore any further.

"I think I should join you in your state of undress, but if you don't mind I'll keep my shoes on!"

It was an attempt to make a joke, both girls giggled politely, humour obviously didn't come naturally to him. They made him stand and with one girl in front and one behind they slowly undressed him. Standing there in their high heels they were both slightly taller. They removed his shirt and for an older man he was in pretty good shape, he had a mass of grey chest hair although it was thinning. He let them take off his trousers and pants and as Karen slipped them down at the front, she was confronted by a small semi stiff cock and a long droopy scrotum with big balls, his pubic hair was quite sparse and the same colour as his chest hair. She sucked very slowly on his limp member and felt it slightly harden in her mouth; she knew it was going to be a tough job but reckoned she was up to the challenge after such a long lay off!

"Take your time Senoras, I'm not in the first flush of youth, I take a lot longer than I used to."

Even now, totally naked, he was quite clearly in control.

"I am going to lay down on the rug: I would like you Sally to position yourself over me so I may indulge you with my tongue and Karen if you could just continue where you left off then, when I give the word, I would like you to swap around, as I said, please take your time."

It was said in such a straightforward manner, it wasn't an order but that is what he wanted and it was clear that he would certainly remain in control, in spite of lying on his back with two women sitting on top of him. He grabbed for a cushion to rest his head on and as he went down Sally couldn't help laughing at the ridiculous site of this old man, Karen and herself all totally nude except for two pairs of shoes between them, she coughed loudly hoping to hide her rather obvious laugh and hoped he hadn't heard.

As he lay down Sally knelt either side of him and positioned her fanny lips next to his mouth: she was rather glad that she had shaved. She felt his hands reach around her bottom and pull her closer to him, she immediately felt his tongue explore her outer lips, he pulled her closer enabling him to gain further access. Karen was gently massaging his balls with one hand while gently licking and sucking on his prick, trying her hardest to get him harder, hard enough so she could sit astride him. She had never had as much trouble as this before, but then again she thought, she had never shagged such an old man! Eventually as her friend began to move backwards and forwards across his face he hardened further and she decided that it was as good as it was going to get and very carefully using both hands to help her, slipped him into her, she felt him immediately respond by thrusting his pelvic area towards her. Sally could now feel his nose against her clitoris and could feel his teeth and tongue working inside her, his hands were moving in time with her movements, she looked down and could only see his closed eyes above her black mass, she knew that even though she hadn't expected to enjoy herself it was, as no doubt Karen would agree, rather better than wanking and also knew, rather surprisingly, she was extremely wet, she laughed inwardly at the thought she might drown him. After only a few minutes he began to moan, quietly at first then louder, it was rather a strange noise but as he moaned the more Sally pressed herself into him. She could feel Karen bouncing up and down on him behind her and thought that even she might be enjoying her first sexual coupling for over a year. All of a sudden he cried out, a muffled noise, probably due to the fact that Sally was sitting on his face, he took his hands away from her bottom, his body and particularly his chest shook and as the spasms subsided he let out a final moan, Sally couldn't believe he had come so soon, all that talk about taking a long time, anyway this was also obviously the sign for them to change positions: she was most concerned what she was going to do with what she imagined would now be a very limp cock while Karen took over her position. If he came so quickly, she bet his recovery time wouldn't be as quick.

She stepped away from him not looking at his face for fear of embarrassment and turned around to see her friend, who was now sitting very still with a fixed stare. Sally's eyes followed her friend's gaze and lying very still below them was the body of Luis. His eyes were still open, staring upwards, his face had gone a pale colour, his lips still very wet from her attention, had a bluish tinge about them.

"He's dead."

"What?"

"He's fucking dead!"

"Oh my God I've suffocated him."

"Don't be an idiot, for someone as bright, you could always be bloody stupid at times he's had a heart attack."

"What the hell are we going to do?"

"Right, as much as I love you like a sister, you get to blow into his mouth and I will work on his chest."

Being both teachers they were fully attuned to resuscitation techniques and like a well-oiled machine they got to work, it's amazing how adrenalin can cure a state of drunkenness almost immediately. They worked on him for fifteen minutes occasionally stopping to see if they could detect any signs of life. It was hopeless he was very dead, if you can be *very* dead. Sally was the first to speak.

"What shall we do now, my God, we're going to get into trouble."

"Well the first thing is that we are not going to panic, now let's think sensibly. Ok there's no need to call an ambulance immediately he's too far gone. Let's quickly get dressed and then I suggest we dress him, put him back on the sofa and shout for the butler."

Although he was a slight man it took them about ten minutes to dress him and drag him onto the sofa. They tried to make him look as natural as possible.

Karen ran out to the landing and started shouting 'Juan' at the top of her voice. Within thirty seconds or so she heard a door opening on the top floor and a light went on. He hurried down the stairs doing up his dressing gown as he did. Karen took him into the drawing room and asked him to ring for an ambulance. He disappeared downstairs and she heard him pick the phone up, she returned to the room and the two girls just looked at each other.

"I could do with a big fucking drink of his brandy, how about you?"

Sally poured out a large amount into their empty wine glasses. The butler re-appeared and said the emergency services would be arriving soon. It hardly seemed a few minutes before they heard the intercom system burst into life and a few moments later two suited gentlemen arrived not looking at all like para medics. They entered the room and introduced themselves: Chief detective something or other and sergeant something else, neither girls were really listening.

"Where's the ambulance?"

"It's on its way. If you would follow me into the dining room, I need to ask you a couple of questions."

He spoke to the other officer who went over to the body, he then ushered the two girls into the dining room.

"I would like you both to tell me what happened here tonight?"

They confirmed their names and address and Karen did most of the talking, Sally occasionally nodding in agreement. It was, they agreed all rather straightforward, they had been in the restaurant and had merely come back for a drink. While they were sitting chatting, he had clutched his chest, made some strange noises and slumped down, the girls immediately shouted for the butler. The Chief didn't say anything, merely acknowledging what they were telling him. In the background they could hear the noise of the para medics taking the body away, then they heard the ambulance drive away.

"I would like you two ladies to accompany me to the station and write a statement of exactly what you have just told me."

He now spoke to them in English even though they both spoke Spanish like natives, Sally thought it was his way of showing superiority, although they were hardly in any position to challenge it. Sally looked at her watch and couldn't believe it was 3.30am – where had the last few hours gone? It was already becoming a horrible dream.

They travelled to the police station in the back of the car in total silence. Once they were inside they were split up and shown into two separate interview rooms and given a piece of paper and asked to write a statement. They both kept exactly to the story they had already told and handed their statements in.

"Thank you ladies, it is now 5am, my officer will take you home and will be back to pick you up at 12 noon once

I have the preliminary post mortem report and I should bring a lawyer with you - goodnight."

They walked into the Karen's apartment slumped down on the sofa and just stared at each other.

"Ok don't look at me like that how on earth was I know he had a weak heart."

Sally remained silent for a moment then got up and headed for the bedroom.

"Can we talk about it in the morning, I can't think straight, why do we need a lawyer if we're not in the shit, big time?"

Karen ignored her.

Sally hardly slept at all, the picture of the dead man filling her head as soon as she tried to close her eyes. Eventually as the dawn came she slipped into a restless sleep. She was awoken by Karen knocking on the door, without waiting for a reply, she walked into the room, uncharacteristically with a dressing gown tightly drawn around her.

"Thought you might like a cup of tea, I think we need to talk. I have been in touch with the legal firm that handled my separation they are going to send one of their partners to meet us at the police office."

They agreed that they needed to stick to their story and agreed to brief the lawyer to that effect. At precisely noon, a uniformed policeman arrived to take them to the police station. The trip to the station took about 30 minutes about twice as long as previously due to heavy traffic. When they arrived they were shown into a small interview room, a moment later the lawyer arrived and introduced himself. Almost at once they were escorted to the Chief's office where they had spent most of the night before and, just as before, he was with the same officer.

"Thank you for coming Senoras." This time he spoke to them in Spanish, he had been matter of fact before but now both girls could feel the hostility. He picked up a file from his desk.

"I have here the preliminary post-mortem report, it is astonishing how forensic science has moved on. Do you know they can even tell what the dead person last ate just from his saliva."

He looked at both women and knew he had scored a direct hit.

"I want you now to both go away and write a new statement. I suggest that we take the unusual step of asking you to write a joint one and hopefully you will be able to jog each other's memory. As the English say I want 'the truth, the whole truth and nothing but the truth, so help you God!' In the meantime, I would like a word with your lawyer in private."

"Is that normal?" Sally looked at Karen as if to say 'shut up; don't make it any worse for us.'

"No, but I think it just maybe to your advantage."

The girls were escorted back to the interview room, given some paper and pens.

"What are we going to write, he knows we had sex with him, all that rubbish about forensics."

"Come on Sally he said that to frighten us, it didn't help that you looked like you had seen a ghost."

The lawyer entered the room looking very grave. He broke the news that the dead man was Luis Garcia one of Spain's top judges, the scourge of ETA, the Basque terrorist organisation. He told them that their previous statements weren't acceptable and they now had to tell the police everything and that potentially they were in big trouble.

"I suggest you write down everything and I mean everything, I will read through it and we will go back in, he wants to see us all in an hour's time."

He left them to it and disappeared saying he wanted a coffee.

"Shit, that's why I thought I recognised him, he's always in the papers and on the T.V."

"I wished you'd recognised him before we got into this mess, right, I don't care what you are going to do I am going to tell the truth."

Sally started to write, Karen looked blankly at the plain walls.

"All right I suppose you are right."

They wrote everything down and didn't leave anything out, after half an hour Sally read it out loud.

"Christ, it sounds like a script for a porn movie, are you sure you had to put in what we actually did, couldn't you have just hinted at it"

When the lawyer returned, Sally handed it him. He read it in silence making no remarks or changing his facial expression.

"You are absolutely certain you haven't left anything out, it is vitally important you put everything in."

"Good in that case we will go and 'face the music'."

Sally didn't like the sound of it and wondered exactly what had been said to him by the police chief, unbeknown to her she was just about to find out.

"Senoras, I believe by now you know who you entertained last night. Have you re-written your statements?"

Their legal representative handed it over. He took it and immediately started to read. About half-way when he got to the bit about resuscitation he said.

"Well at least that explains the broken rib."

He spent at least ten minutes reading and re-reading as if looking for something that wasn't there. Eventually he put it on the desk in front of him, took off his glasses and without saying anything glared at them for what seemed an age.

"You Senoras have managed to do something that ETA has failed to do for the last twenty years." It was as if he was actually accusing them of murder, he continued. "I believe your joint statement in essence now tells the truth of what happened last night and basically is in agreement with the findings of the post-mortem report. Luis Garcia died of a massive heart attack whilst indulging in various sexual acts." He paused before continuing. "So, here is the deal – you two will never, and I mean never, talk about last night to anyone outside of this room, in return we will not prosecute you...."

"For what?"

"Senora Gallas, where would you like me to start? How about attempting to pervert the course of justice, obstructing a police officer, lying to a police officer and............prostitution."

Karen exploded.

"Prostitution?"

He slowly picked up the statement and made as if to read it again then flung it on to his desk.

"So, what would you call it? I suggest you don't interrupt me again until I finish what I am about to say. If ever this got out, that one of Spain's top judges died while being entertained by two hookers," he clearly liked the obvious effect he was having on them. "it would cause a huge embarrassment to the government in Madrid, not to mention playing into the hands of Spain's enemies at home and abroad. You may very well think that this country has very liberal ideals, especially walking along the beach, but let me assure you that the establishment is still very catholic and conservative. The story will be released to the press this afternoon that Senor Luis Garcia died alone at home from a massive heart attack. Let me make it absolutely clear to you both that if the true story gets out, I will personally come and knock on your door and believe me Senoras, there are far more senior and important people than me that would see that you both spent a long time in prison."

Sally shuddered at the thought and was on the verge of breaking down when Karen said.

"But the butler and the chauffeur both know what happened, what if they say something?"

Senora Gallas, please don't concern yourself about them, they are probably two of the most discreet men in the whole country, don't think you are the first two hookers Senor Garcia took back to his villa," he was clearly relishing referring to them as 'hookers', "and anyway, they are employed by the government, they will by now be back on duty looking after the grieving widow at her home in Madrid."

He turned to the lawyer and spoke directly to him.

"Your clients are free to leave but we won't be returning their passports just yet."

As they got up to leave, he spoke once more.

"Oh, I nearly forgot to give you this."

He held a brown envelope in his hand and gave it to Karen.

"The butler asked me to give it to you, something about expenses."

The look on his face was a picture, it said 'game, set and match', and then if to completely rub it in.

"I assume you will be recording it in your records, we don't want to have to add 'tax evasion' to the other offences!"

"Can you forgive me Sally?"

"No, but I could have said no, so I have to take some of the blame."

"I suppose you'll want to go home now?"

"Not right now, first things first I suggest we at least go and spend some of our immoral earnings on a very large drink

"Funny that, that's how it fucking started last night!"

CHAPTER 10

VIVA BENIDORM

Again, they got fairly drunk, but this time on their immoral earnings and were absolutely astonished to find that their 'expenses' amounted to 1,000 euros. They decided in their drunken state that they would spend the rest of their ill-gotten gains on a week in Benidorm, as they originally had agreed to do, never did they think that a dead judge would pay for it, especially one they had a hand in killing.

"Sal, I know a great hotel, it's not on the front but trust me that is an advantage, Miguel and I used to go for the odd weekend, it has entertainment every night, it's full of wrinklies but the food is great and occasionally some decent men come in for a dance. It will still be lively and if you can put up with shaven headed, tattooed British louts and can dodge the motability scooters, it's the place for us."

They didn't wake up until 2pm on the Sunday afternoon, both with sore heads and equally bad tempers.

"Karen, I've been thinking, I've had a great week, well, to be honest not great, I've helped kill a senior member of the Spanish authorities. As a result I've been threatened with imprisonment for tax evasion, prostitution, murder, I've been drunk nearly every day, I really think it's time I went home."

"Come on Sal, I haven't had as much fun since university, I've loved every damned minute but aren't you forgetting something you can't leave the country until you get your passport back."

"I suppose to be honest I haven't much to do if I could get home anyway."

Karen immediately picked up the phone and rang the hotel, five minutes later the booking was confirmed,

Monday to Friday inclusive, bed, breakfast and dinner and two superior rooms as there was a special deal on for mid week bookings.

"Can we agree that we aren't going to get involved with any distinguished, silver haired old gentleman, I'm certainly not going to be on any manhunt."

On Sunday evening Izzie rang.

"Are you coming to Paul's birthday, he's really keen, we both are, come on Sal say you will."

Sally had already decided that after Benidorm she was going to take her time and drive up through Spain then the French Riviera before wending her way through Switzerland and home, she wasn't ready to go home just yet.

"Of course – looking forward to it."
"How's it going?"
"Brilliant." She lied.
"You sound a bit odd, are you ok?"
"Just a bit tired, I'll give you a call tomorrow."

On Monday they took the 'beast' to Benidorm a mere hour's drive from Alicante. The hotel was as Karen had described, on the road parallel to the 'strip', old fashioned but nice, comfortable, four star, not a sign of a motability scooter, tattoo or shaved head anywhere. They were shown to their rooms, 212 and 214 positioned next to each other, they could talk to each other from their balconies. A kingsize bed, a t.v. a rather nice armchair and a desk, almost a suite but not quite. Sally sank onto the bed, she was going to have a restful week, she didn't care what Karen got up to she was not going to be drawn into anything she didn't want to, the last few days had been exciting enough! The phone rang.

"Are you ready, I know a great club, has live music all day."

The Rock Café was well known in Benidorm but somehow on a slightly damp September Monday afternoon, the live duo of a toothless Glaswegian and a young Spanish lothario singing the Proclaimers famous 'five hundred miles' didn't quite hit the mark. After a few bottles of San Miguel things didn't seem so bad and suddenly it was time to go back to the hotel, shower, have a nice dinner and then settle down for the night's entertainment. Sally decided that she would email Maria, it would probably be 'freshers' week at Cambridge and although it seemed a very long time ago, there hadn't been many days when she hadn't thought about her. She didn't know what she thought, she knew she had enjoyed the experience and more than once she had unashamedly masturbated while thinking about what they had done, even now as she started to type she could feel those familiar feelings, those twinges in her lower abdomen an embarrassing dampness in her pants. She knew it wasn't 'right', at no time since puberty had she considered that another woman could turn her on, that was until Maria.

'Hi Maria, you must either be there or about to go. I'm in Spain now I just wanted to wish you all the luck in the world; it doesn't seem that long ago when I started at Uni. Enjoy every moment, believe me it's the best time of your life. I envy you. Let me know how you get on?
  Love Sally x.'

Just writing to her and thinking of her conjured up a mental picture of her lovely form, her smooth tanned eighteen year old body, her gorgeous breasts, dark brown nipples, flat stomach leading down to her perfectly symmetrical, completely shaved mons and prominent clitoris......................stop! She couldn't, she was already fingering herself and knew she wouldn't stop until she was ready. She pulled hard on her breasts and was surprised how sensitive her nipples felt, she needed more, she quickly stripped, grabbed 'Paul' and forced him deep inside her, it slightly hurt but the roughness just added to the moment. She masturbated furiously; at the same time as pushing 'Paul' in and out she pulled and stroked her own clitoris imagining it was Maria's. After five minutes her body was covered in sweat, and when she came she shouted out and surprised herself by the ferocity of it all.

The buffet dinner was surprisingly good, a great selection and plenty of it. They washed it down with a fairly cheap rioja and about 10pm sauntered along to the night's entertainment. Sally was still surprised how late everything seemed to start in Spain; she had forgotten that the Spanish didn't come alive until most British people were thinking about their beds. The entertainment was a live three-piece band with a girl singer, it was ok especially as it was free but eventually they tired and couldn't be bothered to stay for the dancing and went to bed. Sally looked at her emails, half hoping there might be a response from Maria but she was disappointed, there was one from an old teacher friend bringing her up to date with what was happening at school but that was all. She considered texting her but then decided against it, clearly there was and never could have been a future in it and anyway what on earth was she thinking about?

The next few days carried on pretty much as the previous one. Got up late, had breakfast, walked along the promenade dodging the motability scooters and baby buggies, stopping for a drink and then usually, not always, ending up in the old village and always the same tapas bar, the one all the locals used and thankfully very few of the tourists. They would then retrace their steps as the sun went down, calling in at the same old bars where live entertainment was normally in full swing, pacing themselves on the alcohol front, limiting the alcoholic drinks to just one per bar and more often than not a coke or coffee. The week flew by and it gave Sally time to catch her breath to begin to enjoy the freedom of no work, no school and no students to worry about. She planned her trip home, she aimed to get back by mid-October this would leave her about a month at home before she set off to Zurich again for Paul's birthday on the 15th of November. She had decided to stay away from the 'pay' roads and as time was of no consequence would use the local roads. She intended spending more time in Barcelona then slowly working her way around the Riviera, Marseille, Montpelier, Sete, St Tropez, Cannes then on to Nice staying at the Negresco. She knew it would be an 'arm and a leg', but she could afford it, her and Dave had stayed there many years before. He had arranged it as a surprise not long after they were married telling her that they were going to London, as they were driving up the M4 he suddenly pulled into Heathrow and sprung the surprise. They hired a car and toured around the beautiful countryside in Haute Provence ending up one day at the top of the Verdon Gorge at a little place called Moustier St. Marie, they had always vowed that one day they would return, they never did, this is where Sally decided she would spend the last few days before heading home.

In a moment of madness the girls decided to spend their last day at the water park just a few miles from Benidorm, they would be kids again. Luckily the weather was still very warm during the day even though the water has lost some of its summer warmth. They spent all day there going on every ride, slide and basically just having a good time. By the time they got back they were worn out and decided they would head for the Rock café, listen to the toothless duo, get ready to go out on the town and make the most of their last night together.

Returning to her room for a shower and change before the evening's entertainment Sally checked her emails. There were quite a few and the one she really wanted was there, her heart skipped a beat and she thought how ridiculous it was.

'Hi Sally,

Sorry for not coming back sooner, I spent a few days in Cambridge with a friend just finding my way around, I don't start until next weekend; you know how it is, we only have three eight week terms and all my friends have already been at Uni for at least three weeks, to tell the truth I'm rather bored. Mum and Dad are on holiday.....again and guess what? I've finished with my boyfriend, he started to get a bit possessive, wanting to know where I was and what I was doing, I think he was very jealous that I'm off to Cambridge, anyway, just think of all the men I can have a go at University? Trouble is Sally I'm already missing sex, I know I used to go weeks without it as he lived In Switzerland, but perhaps the thought that I can't have it, is bugging me. Have you met any nice men? Let me know, I really miss you. Do you realise that this is the longest period I haven't seen you since I started senior school?

Must dash, most of my friends are home from Uni this weekend and we're going clubbing in Bournemouth, don't suppose I'll be home until the early hours. Keep emailing it was really great to hear from you.

Love and kisses Maria.xxxxxxx.'

She was excited by the email and secretly knew why, the thoughts of a couple of months before were still very sharp in her mind. When they met for dinner even Karen couldn't help noticing how happy she was.

"You seem pleased with yourself I could almost believe you were looking forward to leaving me tomorrow."

"Course I'm not, who else could I have killed a judge with, got horribly drunk every other night with, spent a fortune with, went to a children's water park with, but at least I can pick up my passport when I get back?"

"You know Sally I want to get laid tonight and not by some old age pensioner like last Friday."

"Please don't count me in, last week was enough to put me off sex for ever!"

They headed for dinner, took their time and instead of the usual one bottle managed to get through a gin and tonic for starters then two bottles of Spanish merlot, by the time they got to the night's entertainment and dance they were already feeling a little unsteady, but they were hardened drinkers and immediately had a cocktail as soon as they arrived. Because it was a Friday the place was full, not only with residents but the middle-class locals who obviously came most Friday evenings. They were both asked to dance on a number of occasions, which they did but each time by men at least old enough to be their fathers.

"Jesus, Sally it's like an old folk's home!"

Sally couldn't deny it, she looked around the bar, they certainly had lowered the average age. There were however two young lads sitting around the bar, she whispered to Karen.

"There you are girl, they seem a couple of likely lads they can't be more than 20."

Clearly Spanish in their looks; both were reasonably good looking and from where the girls were sitting, seemed to have good bodies.

"They'll do, come on Sally lets go and ask them to dance."

"I told you, I'm not interested, leave me out."

"I can't ask them on my own, please, it's only a dance."

Sally really didn't want to, but it was *only* a dance.

They were taken aback, they obviously had never been asked to dance by women before and for a moment it looked like they might refuse. Karen asked them in English, not wanting to let on that both were fluent in Spanish and thought it gave them a better chance of success. They agreed and took to the floor, Karen partnered the shorter of the two who was still slightly taller than her, whilst Sally was surprised that her partner was a good four or five inches taller. He was a very good mover and she found that she just followed him around, not quite sure what steps she was attempting, but somehow as with all good dancers he guided her around the dance floor and it was as if they had been partners for years. He was very good looking and in different circumstances she might have been turned on by being in such close proximity but the thought of having a casual relationship was far from her thoughts. After about twenty minutes on the floor Sally was tiring and said that she would like a drink. They managed to find a table and being the gentleman that he obviously was, went to the bar and brought back a large brandy. Karen on the other hand was still dancing and to Sally's astonishment did a very passable tango, they continued for another twenty minutes before finally joining them at the table. The boys command of English was very good but nowhere near as fluent as the girls were in Spanish, however they didn't let on and kept up the pretence that they were just there on holiday for a few days. As the night wore on they drank more and danced; Sally recognised the 'old Karen', the 'predatory Karen', the 'university Karen' and could tell that she had decided that her and her new partner would end up having sex. Sally had observed her for three years and knew the signs. She looked at her watch and was amazed that it was 1.30am, she wanted to go to bed and plan for the morning. She signalled to Karen that she wanted to talk to her and both girls headed for the cloakroom.

"I'm buggered, I'm going to bed."

"You can't, I'm on to a winner, come on Sally I already know that Jose fancies you, Javier told me, don't leave me in the lurch. They are best friends, apparently they've known each other since they were boys, went to University together, if you go they'll both go."

"Sorry but I'm not interested, I really don't want to, they have been delightful company and I'll go and say goodnight to them."

"You really haven't changed have you?"

Sally ignored the comment knowing that after a few too many Karen could get a bit aggressive and went back to the bar.

"Thank you both for a lovely night but I have a long way to drive tomorrow and I'm off to bed."

The both stood, kissed her on both cheeks and wished her a safe journey home.

She was so pleased to have the sanctuary of her bedroom she wasn't at all tired using it as an excuse to escape. Slipping off her clothes she put on her dressing gown, poured yet another glass of red, decided that she'd spoil herself with a cohiba esplendido and went out onto her balcony. The road was still busy, she looked at her watch, it was 2am but with the amount of traffic one could have believed it was the middle of the day, Benidorm was still buzzing. The air was still warm and as she sipped her wine and smoked her cigar she felt very at ease with the world, she had had a great two weeks with Karen but was ready to move on and was looking forward to her next stage of travelling. Suddenly she heard her text messaging tone, who on earth was texting her at this time of the morning? Retrieving it from her room she heard voices from her friend's room next door, she couldn't hear what was being said but there was definitely a man's voice, or possibly two, just as well she thought she wasn't ready for bed yet, it was probably going to be a long noisy night!

'Are you still awake'?

She looked at the detail – Maria. Instantly she felt butterflies in her tummy, she knew how absolutely silly, childish her feelings were but there was nothing she could do about it. She took a long draw on her cigar deciding whether to answer or not.

'Yes.'
'Just got in, rather the worse for wear, going to bed.....missing you so much.'

Sally was in a real quandary, what happened in the summer was a 'one-off' she could almost feel where this was going. Maria was drunk and *she* wasn't exactly sober, but by God she fancied her; the butterflies were spreading, she knew it was as a result of the adrenalin now being released, she took another drink and a puff on her cohiba.

'Are you still there, I'm in bed now, wish it was that day in August. Can I come and stay again?'
　'Anytime.'
　'Do you ever think about me?'
　'Yes.'
　'In the way I'd like you to?'
　'I don't know, what way would you like me to think of you?'
　'Sexually.'

Sally knew this had already gone too far, she decided that she wouldn't respond straight away hoping that Maria would probably fall asleep.

Karen took a shower, dried quickly then walked into the bedroom naked. The two young men stood there looking embarrassed.
　"Go on then, get your kit off and have a shower, I'll wait."
　She climbed in between the sheets as first one then the other disappeared in the bathroom. She heard the shower being turned on and what seemed only to be a couple of seconds Jose appeared with a towel around his waist.
　"Come on get into bed with me.'
　He did as he was told, dropping the towel as he did so. Karen caught a glimpse of his erect phallus, she liked what she saw. Instantly she reached out for him and touched him.
　"Have you got a condom?"
　He shook his head.
　"Then be careful, I don't want to get pregnant."

He took this as a signal to start and almost at once rolled on top of her and she could feel his clumsy attempts to enter her, obviously he hadn't heard of foreplay. She helped him find her, guiding him with her hand until suddenly finding her moist opening, shoved his member inside her. Karen grimaced at the sudden intrusion, she, or more importantly her vagina wasn't quite ready to accommodate him and she slightly pushed him away. He, however, was quite oblivious and continued to thrust in and out. Karen knew it wouldn't be long and within only a couple of minutes she felt him begin to climax and pushed him away. He came, shooting his stuff over her stomach and into her pubic hair. As shags went, she thought, that wasn't one of the best, she still wasn't properly moist. She left him lying on the bed and went to the shower, standing there was Javier looking at himself in the mirror, he hadn't seen her come in, his cock was curved like a banana and he was holding it in his hand. Ignoring his embarrassment, she went behind him and cupping his balls with one hand she took his 'banana' in the other and gently started to wank him off whilst they both looked at themselves in the mirror. She slowly pulled his foreskin back as far as it would go exposing a lovely pinky brown head, she used her thumb, stroking around the rim and at the same time gently squeezing his fast-shrinking balls. He was very hairy and well muscled, quite a six pack just above his pubis. She rather liked him and wanted him inside her as soon as she could, no need for any foreplay, she'd already had that; she pulled him into the shower, turning the water on and without any warning put one foot on the small shower seat allowing him easy access; putting one hand around his neck she pulled him to her kissing him fully on the lips, with her free hand she rubbed her cunt in time with his movements. They rocked backwards and forwards, she was having trouble breathing as the water cascaded over her hair and face, but this only added to the excitement. Without any of her normal warning signs, she came, taking them both by surprise, it was short, sharp and noisy, she left him in the shower to finish himself off, quickly dried and walked back into the bedroom.

Sally didn't answer, she was in that state between waking and sleeping, feeling incredibly relaxed; she closed her eyes and imagined Maria lying on her bed. Suddenly the text messaging alerted her, she reached for the phone and saw that she had a multimedia message waiting. She opened it.........there in glorious technicolor detail was a picture of Maria's very naked, pink, moist fanny, legs wide apart, her left hand resting on her thigh. Suddenly, Sally felt very predatory, this girl had been her student, was only just turned nineteen, morally, ethically..........the same guilty thoughts she'd had previously came flooding back, but try as she might she couldn't deny her innermost feelings, her hand slipped down inside the covers and within five minutes, her immediate passion extinguished, she fell into a heavy sleep.

CHAPTER 11

END OF AN ERA

Leaving Karen and promising to catch up with her again in the New Year, Sally very slowly made her way back home, taking a couple of weeks to wind her way through Spain, France and Switzerland stopping in some places she had planned but missing out others, unfortunately the Negresco was full, in retrospect perhaps it was a blessing, certainly it had saved her a fortune and it would only have re-awakened her feelings for Dave. She finally arrived home the second week in October and amazingly enough hadn't had any further sexual adventures although she felt she probably wasn't due any more for a while when considering the previous 12 months! Opening the door to her cottage she was hit with the same overwhelming loneliness of the first few months after losing Dave, she had been far too occupied for the last couple of months to dwell on her situation, but now all alone in an empty house it was inescapable. She wasn't due to go on her travels again until mid-November when she had promised to drive to Zurich again and celebrate Paul's 45th birthday, she really hoped she could keep busy until then to keep her from sinking into what she knew could be a very dark place.

She didn't arrive until late on Friday night, the traffic and weather from the channel port had been horrible, then again it was a silly idea to travel on a Friday in any country, the night everybody wants to get home to their families. Izzie let her in and immediately gave her a drink, thought you might need one.
"Has it been a difficult journey?
"Yes, dreadful, but I'm here now and it's amazing how a kiss and a hug from my best friend and a decent gin and tonic can pick you up - where's birthday boy?"

"He's just rang from the office he'll be about half an hour, anyway he's not 45 until tomorrow, I hope he's in a better mood than last weekend, work is really getting him down. Fancy something to eat?"

"No thanks."

Sally seemed to have gone off food the last few days and hadn't eaten very much, somehow, she had temporarily lost her appetite. They sat and chatted, Sally telling her about Karen and Benidorm, but not telling her anything about 'the judge', the thought of languishing in a Spanish jail filled her with total horror. Izzie basically brought her up to date with the family, her dad had been over for a week, which nearly drove her mad and although Paul was in a stress over work, sex was still totally awesome.

"Awesome?"

"Ok, fucking awesome."

They were both still laughing when Paul let himself in, he kissed Izzie passionately on the lips and then gave Sally a more sisterly hug.

"Come on then, what's so funny?"

"Sally has just told me what she's bought you for your birthday." She lied.

"I know what I'd like."

There was certainly no ambiguity about his response.

"You'll just have to wait and see."

Sally realised that although they all knew and hoped what they would both give him for his birthday, she hadn't actually bought him a present. She would pay for dinner the following night, that could be her gift. After another hour or so Paul excused himself and went to bed. Sally and Izzie, as they always did when they hadn't actually seen each other for a while sat up until the early hours, they never quite knew what they talked about, most of the time it was utter trivia but it didn't matter, they were best friends and this is what best friends did, other things best friends didn't necessarily do, but that was a very different friendship!

She woke up feeling distinctly under the weather, her head ached, unusually not through drink as she had only had a couple of drinks all day, but worst of all she felt very sick. It gradually got worse until she knew she had to go to the bathroom, she was very sick and hoped that her hosts couldn't hear her vomiting. After about ten minutes she felt well enough to leave the en-suite and crawl back into bed, it was only 7.30am and hopefully she hadn't woken them. She was sick a further three times and after each episode crawled back into bed feeling totally wretched. What had she eaten? The only thing she could think of was the moules and frites she had the previous lunchtime (probably not the best decision in a country that was landlocked and not known for its seafood), it was always possible with shellfish that the odd one caused a big problem. At 9.30 the door opened and in walked Izzie with a mug of tea.

"Are you ok, you look a bit peeky."

"No, I'm fine, just didn't sleep very well."

"Believe it or not Paul has had to go into the office, at least he's back in the Zurich branch now, he's really pissed off, especially on his birthday!"

Sally was secretly pleased, she would have hated to spoil his birthday, hopefully she would get over the bout of food poisoning; she was already feeling better and knew that an hour earlier she certainly couldn't have faced a cup of tea. By 10.30 she was almost back to normal and after a shower joined Izzie in the kitchen.

"He's just rang, apparently storm in a teacup, he'll be home by lunchtime. I thought we would have a bit of a late breakfast and then he said he'd like to go to the sports club for a game of tennis before going out this evening, but only if you are up to it?"

Sally didn't feel brilliant, but the sickness had disappeared, and the exertions of the morning had left her feeling a bit tired, but not wanting to spoil his birthday she readily agreed.

They played a few games each, a sort of 'round robin', Sally was beaten quite easily by them both but excused herself by saying that she had done very little exercise for the last couple of months, which wasn't entirely without foundation. Both Izzie and Paul seemed keen on a sauna, Sally didn't, but went with the flow. Moments later she found herself looking at him and knew she wanted him, she wanted his fat cock in every available orifice, she knew her thoughts were shameless but didn't care, if it was good for them and it worked, then fine. By the time they got back to the apartment she felt back to normal and was glad that she had played tennis, clearly whatever she'd eaten was out of her system and was looking forward to dinner and for the first time all day felt quite hungry. She knew what was expected of her later and with that in mind she trimmed and shaved, it was odd how she had changed over the last few months and although she still liked her thick pubic bush, she loved the feeling of her smoothly shaved lips and wondered what Dave would have thought, if only they had talked about it, they never talked about anything like that!

They started off with a couple glasses of champagne at home before the taxi picked them up and took them to the restaurant. Sally knew that it was probably the most expensive restaurant in Zurich, but the chef had two Michelin stars and that didn't come cheap. They had wanted to pay but Sally had insisted and finally they gave in, but only because it was a birthday present.

"It's really expensive."

They had no idea what she was worth, it was something they didn't discuss at all and it wasn't something that well brought up people do. Her parents had never talked about money and she was of the same ilk, it was all rather private.

It was on reflection probably one of the best meals she had ever had, each course was an explosion of taste, apart from anything else the plate or dish or bowl could have been framed, they were all a marvellous work of art. It seemed that each course was complemented with a different glass of wine, not a lot but it was as though the combination of flavours had been perfectly matched. It was without doubt an experience that she wouldn't forget in a hurry, all memories of the morning's sickness had long since disappeared. They finished with a very old aged brandy and a coffee, the only thing missing for Sally was a cigar, but she didn't feel it appropriate, however much she would have liked one. When she took the bill she'd wished she'd had one, if only to calm her nerves. 635 Swiss francs would have fed her and probably a family of four for a couple of months but although to many people the amount would have been an outrage, she didn't regret one franc, it was quite simply a fantastic experience. She paid the bill and gave a reasonably generous tip taking it up to a round 700. As they left the restaurant Paul planted a big kiss fully on her lips.

"Thanks Sal, but you are our guest and I feel embarrassed."

"Happy birthday, it's not every day you're 45 and I'm sure you'll find a way to make it up to me."

She knew what she was saying was a tease, but it was far easier with a few drinks on board.

"Don't worry, we both will."

The taxi was already waiting for them. They all clambered into the back he was in the middle flanked by both girls. He said something in German to the driver and they sped off homewards. There was without question a slightly charged atmosphere, an air of expectancy. It was dark in the cab only occasionally lit up by the streetlights as they went beneath them. Sally could see the bulge in his trousers and didn't know whether she had the courage to start something right there in the cab. They had taken to small talk when Izzie grabbed his belt and almost in one move undid the top of his trousers and unzipped him exposing his nearly erect penis. Sally said nothing, looking at both of them clearly expecting her friend to make the next move. She didn't disappoint and immediately reached over, took Sally's hand and together they touched and stroked his now fully erect knob.

"Happy birthday darling, think of this as an aperitif."

She kissed him on the cheek. Not to be outdone Sally kissed his other cheek.

"Happy birthday darling, think of this as 'a pair of teeth'."

There was silence in the cab; Paul kept his eyes on the rear-view mirror almost daring the driver not to look. Izzie giggled not sure what to say, Paul didn't say anything: Sally gagged on his now very erect cock.

"We're here."

Izzie announced their arrival by a few hundred yards giving them both a chance to sort themselves out. It was a huge struggle to get his prick back inside his boxers and do his trousers up, they were now all laughing out loud and didn't care what the taxi driver thought was going on. Paul paid him and gave him a very handsome tip, he said thanks and gave Paul a knowing look!

Once inside there was no foreplay, as they walked towards the lounge they had already started to take their clothes off and by the time Izzie turned on the lamp and put on some music they were all naked. As they lay down Sally immediately carried on where she had left off only a few moments before, taking him in her mouth, using her teeth, covering his circumcised head in her saliva, she had no idea where her friend was, if like before then probably seeing to herself while watching. After a short time she felt him move and then she felt her legs being parted, tenderly her smooth lower lips being parted and like a bee drinking nectar from the honeypot, felt his tongue darting in and out of her vagina, she was shocked, because if she ever had a complaint about his lovemaking it was his slight roughness when he was giving cunnilingus, she had never complained though and thought that Izzie must have been giving him lessons. She felt his fingers now enter her, at the same time his thumb rubbing her delicate bud, she knew she didn't want to come yet this was just too delicious. His thrusting became ever more urgent, he moved slightly to try and position himself better and as he moved Sally looked up and could see quite clearly Izzie's legs wrapped tightly around her husbands neck and then to her total astonishment, realised it was her friend who was licking and kissing her and very firmly inside her. Rather than revulsion she was totally turned on by the new sequence of events. The three bodies made a perfect triangle on the lounge floor, clearly the new situation suited them all. Paul was now grunting loudly, and Sally got ready to finish him off, not wishing to swallow this time, she grabbed his spongy head with her thumb and forefinger and squeezed him until he jerked and spurted over her shoulder and the carpet. He lay still for a moment and Sally daren't move letting Izzie continue, not wanting her to stop. Eventually he stood up and very gently he positioned his wife's legs towards Sally's very responsive mouth, there was no question what he wanted and to his absolute pleasure he wasn't at all disappointed. The two girls immediately went into a sixty-nine position, but with Izzie on top and as Sally rolled onto her back Izzie took the opportunity to fully open Sally's lips giving her complete and unrestricted access to her glorious fanny. Not to be left out she positioned her knees either side of Sally's head and as she did Paul reached down and put a large pillow under Sally's neck helping her to lick and explore his wife's very ripe cunt. Sally kissed Izzie's beautifully trimmed labia and, as she did smelt her ripeness, not that she needed an aphrodisiac but as she breathed in the heady combination of her friend's perfume and sex juice, knew her own climax was not far away. They both pressed harder, their tongues and fingers working overtime, almost trying to convey to the other what each of them wanted from the coupling. Sally was about to come but as she did, she knew her friend was also on the brink and tried harder to help her friend. They came together in one writhing mass on the floor, their guttural moans, shrieks, panting and rasping breaths drowning out the music. No-one moved for what seemed an age until eventually Izzie stood up and walked out. Paul just looked at Sally not saying anything, Sally wasn't surprised to see that had he not only recovered but seemed bigger than ever. She knew what he wanted but felt totally spent.

"I know it's your birthday, but I need time to recover, just don't lose 'it' until I'm ready."

Izzie was obviously thinking along the same lines and still naked she carried in three large gin and tonics.

"Thought we might need re-hydrating?"

Still sitting on the floor and with not a trace of embarrassment they drank their drinks, each of them propped up against a seat: they listened to the music, dozed, they didn't need to talk. Eventually Izzie disappeared again only to return seconds later with a bottle of lube and a dildo. She walked over to Sally, motioned her to stand up, squirted a generous helping of 'tingling mint' onto the palm of her hand, "Paul said you weren't keen on pina colada", and with the same gentleness as before massaged it into Sally's genital area, taking care to make sure every bit of her was nice and moist, both inside and out, at the same time kissing her fully on the mouth. She then walked towards her husband and anointing his balls and prick then moved away. Sally looked at Paul's manhood now shiny and glistening in the half light and was grateful that although temporarily losing 'it', 'it' had returned and was obviously ready for service. The two lovers moved to a position on the floor, while the concubine took her lube and dildo and took the seat that would give her the best vantage point. There was no urgency as in the past, there was no need and they were both tired. Slowly he opened her up with his fingers and then with deliberate strokes gently entered her; they moved in time, it was what she and Dave would have called a 'long leisurely fuck', the sort of thing they used to do on a Sunday morning. She loved Paul, in fact she loved Izzie as well, not like she had loved Dave but a lustful love, it was definitely a sexual love, but she didn't care, she wanted it to last forever. They were as one, they were totally oblivious to the stranger sitting in the armchair rocking back and forwards. He came but she didn't, she didn't care it was time she went to bed, and it was time he went back to his wife.

Something made her wake up, the nausea had returned, she obviously had a bad tummy bug, she only just made it to the toilet, she vomited quite violently then crawled back to bed and noted that it was still only 8am, she had only been in bed for about four hours. This pattern of events was repeated for the next couple of hours, finally exhausted she fell into a deep sleep and only woke when Izzie brought in a cup of tea at 12.15. The last thing she wanted was for Izzie to know she was unwell she really didn't want to spoil the weekend.

"Sleep ok?"

"Yes thanks, great, don't remember coming to bed." She lied.

"You?"

"Fantastic, not much sleep though! Paul said it was the best birthday he has ever had. Said he couldn't wait until it's mine. We thought we'd go for a walk to the club, somehow we're not very hungry, how about you?"

"Sounds great, I'll get up and have a shower."

The arrangement suited Sally as the last thing she wanted to do was eat but at least she felt better, she really hoped that was the end of her tummy upset.

The rest of the day was a relaxed affair; they had a couple of drinks at the club, although Sally stayed away from alcohol and when they got back had a sandwich. They didn't speak about the previous night, but then again married couples didn't often discuss the sex they had the night before and the three of them had become a 'married couple'. Paul was off early the next morning to the office and Sally had decided that she would start her journey home at the same time, hopefully missing the Monday morning Zurich traffic. Sally set her alarm for 5.45am hoping to get away at 6.30am, the same time as Paul's taxi was booked.

Opening her eyes as the alarm went off, she was delighted that she didn't feel like the last two mornings. She showered, had a coffee, although not feeling like anything to eat and after goodbyes and promising to see them both again before Christmas she was on the road by 6.40am. It was quite busy, and it took nearly an hour before she was heading north on the A1. The traffic was also very heavy on the motorway. Quite suddenly she started to feel unwell again, she wanted to stop but had somehow got stuck in the fast lane with an unbroken line of traffic on the inside lanes, she wanted to be sick, she had awful pains in her lower abdomen, she had to stop and due to the intense pain was beginning to feel faint. She tried to move to the inside lane but a large Mercedes van blocked her course, she suddenly saw it and swerved back onto the fast lane, but over controlling she let the front left wheel hit the central reservation, at 110 kph she never stood a chance of rescuing the situation, 'the beast' turned sidewards and immediately started to roll over. The last thing Sally remembered was a loud bang as the airbag went off and then the terrifying sound of breaking glass and then complete and utter silence.

Izzie was at home listening to the local radio when she heard that the A1 was shut and was likely to remain shut for some time. She looked at her watch and thought that Sally would have been well past that point by now, she hoped she wouldn't be held up but she wasn't on a strict time line and certainly hadn't bothered booking a ferry, at this time of year there were plenty of spaces. She and Paul had enjoyed the weekend more than they could have possibly imagined and couldn't imagine a time when Sally wasn't going to be in their lives. The two of them had stayed in the lounge long after Sally had retired, and their sex lives had taken on a totally new and exciting dimension. There was no way even a year earlier she could ever have imagined doing what she did but coming late to it she almost wished she'd done it earlier. It had certainly re-invigorated their marriage; she bet the results of counselling would never have suggested such a thing. She made a mental note to ring her friend at the weekend and organise a get together over Christmas, although as the boys would be home from boarding school, they may have to wait until *her* birthday in February.

It took over an hour to cut her from the wreckage, amazingly apart from a couple of shunts behind, no-one else was injured. Even the occupants of the large Mercedes Van that had been on the inside lane were uninjured, although having no chance of missing her had smashed into the side of 'the beast' as it came to a standstill. She was, luckily for her, unconscious: 'the beast' had ended up on its roof straddling the two inside lanes. The fire and rescue service had a job getting through the heavy traffic and the first firemen on the scene were totally astonished that they found someone still alive in the mangled, twisted lump of metal that had once been a camper van. It was vital they got her to a hospital quickly, although the doctor in attendance had managed to stabilise her condition. The helicopter only took ten minutes to get her back to the accident and trauma unit in the Zurich University Hospital: more used to treating skiing injuries even they were shocked at her apparent injuries and two teams immediately started working to try and stem the internal bleeding, they needed to work fast as her life was very slowly slipping away.

Izzie had just put down the phone to her husband, who as usual, was 'pissed off' at the incompetence's of his staff in the Berlin office. The phone rang again, she looked at the clock, it was just approaching 7pm and thought it would be her dad as he usually rang about that time. She considered ignoring it and ringing back, but as with most dutiful daughters, guilt kicked in and after a few rings she picked it up.

"Hello, is that Mrs Thomas?"

"Yes."

"Do you have a friend, Mrs Sally Matthews?"

"Yes."

"I'm afraid she has been involved in an accident and you are on her passport as the person to contact in case of a problem."

"Sorry, what are you saying?"

"Mrs Matthews has been involved in a very serious accident and she is here at the Zurich University Hospital. She is in a very critical condition and still undergoing surgery, we won't know anymore for at least twenty-four hours. Please take this number and ring again tomorrow afternoon and ask for the duty supervisor, I'm sorry but I can't give you any further information."

"Thank you."

She put the phone down; she wasn't sure what to do. There was only one thing she could do and that was to ring Paul. He didn't answer either his office number or mobile, she knew he would be locked in a meeting, or more likely at a local bar. She left a message on both phones and hoped he would call her back; she was in a total state of shock.

Over the next twenty-four hours the exact details became clear, Paul took time out from the office to be with Izzie and together they went to the hospital.

"She is in intensive care; she has serious internal and head injuries. We can't say anymore than that, the next forty-eight hours will be critical. Does she have any family?"

"I'll ring her parents they are quite old but I'll try and get hold of them tonight."

"Thanks for coming in, do you want to sit with her?"

They shook their heads. They decided they didn't, instead they wanted to go home and ring her parents.

"We will keep you informed; if her condition deteriorates, we will let you know."

After a few hours ringing and leaving messages they gave up, Izzie remembered that Sally had said something about them going on holiday, they didn't know what else to do, but perhaps the fact they couldn't get hold of them for the time being was a good thing. Izzie knew Sally's mother and father quite well, meeting them on many occasions when they visited Sally although she hadn't seen her father since he had had a heart attack and wondered how they would take the news, she would keep trying until she spoke to them.

Over the next few days her condition went from critical to critical, but stable. She was under very heavy sedation to keep her in a medically induced coma, giving time for the swelling on her brain to subside. Izzie visited every day and sat with her, Paul had gone back to work as there was very little he could do, they still couldn't get hold of Sally's parents. As each day passed there seemed little change until on the Monday afternoon, a week to the day since the accident, Izzie arrived only to find the screens around Sally's bed and feared the worst. She was well known to the staff and they were now less formal with her calling her by her Christian name.

"Hi Izzie, don't look so worried, Sally woke up this morning and has uttered a few words. You can go in but please no more then five minutes, it's going to be a slow recovery."

Ten minutes later they let her in, as she took her seat next to her friend, Sally opened her eyes and smiled at her, they didn't say anything, but Izzie with tears in her eyes, squeezed her friends hand, somehow talking wasn't necessary. Over the next few days Sally gradually began to talk more although it was difficult as she was still very heavily bandaged and seemed to have tubes coming from every part of her body. When Paul arrived on Friday evening he was amazed at her progress and although she was still groggy with morphine managed to have a conversation with him. Izzie had managed to speak to Sally's parents that afternoon; they had been on a cruise and had only returned the previous evening. Izzie managed to put them off flying out immediately and had played down her friend's condition, she agreed that she would pick them up from the airport on the Tuesday afternoon and they would of course stay with her.

On Monday quite a few of her tubes were removed and they also took off the bandages around her head, she was talking far more and Izzie told her, in an effort to make her laugh, that she looked like she was from a horror movie. They also moved her to a less acute ward. She was looking forward to seeing her parents on Wednesday and each day she seemed to be getting stronger. On the Tuesday morning they told her that the consultant would like to talk to her and would she like her friend to be with her.

"That sounds ominous?"

"No, it's something we always ask."

The answer didn't sound too convincing; however, she decided that she would prefer to hear any bad news on her own.

"You are a very lucky young woman, you sustained serious head and internal injuries, but apart from a few scars and you may suffer some memory loss, you should in time make nearly a full recovery."

"Nearly?"

"I think you may possibly have a limp for the rest of your life as your left leg took most of the impact, however…….."

Sally knew there was something else.

"Yes?"

"However, I'm afraid I do have some rather bad news." He hesitated again. "I'm terribly sorry but we couldn't save your unborn child."

She heard what he said but didn't understand. She looked at him blankly. He thought she may not have heard and very slowly said it again.

"We couldn't save your child, I'm very sorry and………

As if there could be an 'and'?

"And due to your very serious internal injuries, you won't be able to have any further children."

She had been carrying her best friend's husband's baby!

"Have you any questions?"

Without thinking, her mind in a total blur she just looked at him and said as if it were the most natural thing in the world after been given such earth-shattering news.

"Does that mean I can't have sex again?"

The question took him completely by surprise and thought it might be as a result of severe shock, he had seen it before.

"I, I,….I don't see why not, I'm sure that everything in that department will be back in order - eventually."

"Good." Was all she could say.

He left saying he would call in the next day to see how she was. He was sure that after it had sunk in, she would have a few other more practical questions for him.

She stared into space, she had been carrying Paul's baby, she didn't know how she felt, it was a very weird feeling, it would have been complicated and she didn't know whether she would have made a good mother, but now she would never find out. It must have been when she was with him at the beginning of September, when Izzie had to conveniently disappear, she obviously wasn't as careful as she should have been, the foetus must have been about 10 weeks old. She didn't feel any particular remorse and knew morally she should have done, but it was never meant to happen, having sex with him was recreational not procreational. She gingerly moved her hand under the sheets, past the many dressings and then inside her surgical pants, her hand briefly wandered as if not really wanting to find out what had happened down there, everything felt reasonably normal, if not a little prickly as her once thick bush had clearly been shaved, although everything still hurt like hell - *she* wouldn't and certainly no-one else would be playing down there for a while!

"Your parents are outside, can they come in?"

She burst into tears, she didn't know why but she suddenly felt terribly alone, terribly vulnerable, terribly frightened, she could only wonder what the future might hold.

Lightning Source UK Ltd.
Milton Keynes UK
UKHW010636091120
373072UK00001B/24